P9-DBZ-230

"The world must know what happened, and never forget."

– Dwight D. EISENHOWER, General, U.S. Army

Supreme Commander of the Allied Forces during World War II

THE LAST GOOD WAR

The Faces and Voices of World War II

Thomas SANDERS
Text by Veronica KAVASS
Introduction by Hampton SIDES

Edited by Katrina FRIED & Gavin O'CONNOR Designed by Gregory WAKABAYASHI

Published by Welcome Books New York

This book would not have been possible without
the support of Belmont Village Senior Living.

Published in 2010 by Welcome Books®
An imprint of Welcome Enterprises, Inc.
6 West 18th Street, New York, NY, 10011
(212) 989-3200; fax (212) 989-3205
www.welcomebooks.com

Publisher: Lena Tabori
President: H. Clark Wakabayashi
Editors: Katrina Fried and Gavin O'Connor
Editorial Assistant: Emily Green
Designer: Gregory Wakabayashi

Library of Congress Cataloging-in-Publication Data on file

ISBN: 978-1-59962-085-5

First Edition
10 9 8 7 6 5 4 3 2 1

PRINTED IN CHINA

For further information about this book please visit online: www.welcomebooks.com/lastgoodwar

Cover: **Dick FRANKEL, Officer, U.S. Navy Signal Corps**

Preceding spread: **Harold COOK, Chief Machinist's Mate, U.S. Naval Reserve** Opposite: **Raymond MITCHELL, Private First Class, U.S. Army**

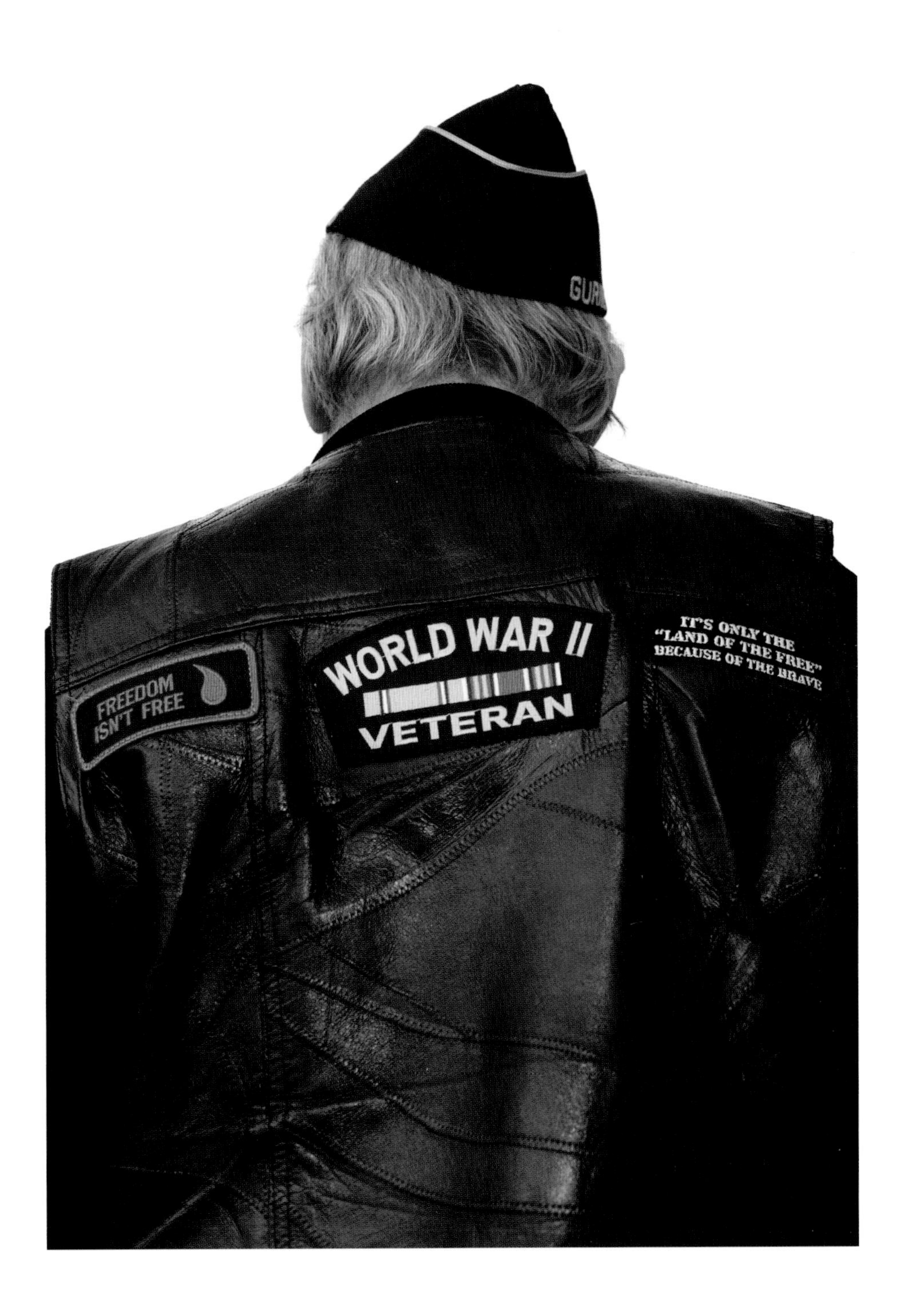

This book is dedicated to all American veterans and soldiers, especially to those who do not make it home.

—T.S.

INTRODUCTION Hampton SIDES

IT WAS THE GREAT ORAL HISTORIAN STUDS TERKEL WHO CALLED IT "THE GOOD WAR." That was just a figure of speech, of course. All war is emphatically, horrifically bad—World War II especially. There was nothing "good" about it.

Yet there was something about the men and women who fought in it, something about the times in which they lived and the grace and fortitude with which they plunged themselves into service. Never before or since have Americans rallied so forcefully around a single cause. The colossal challenge of defeating Hitler on one side of the planet, and Tojo on the other, summoned qualities the nation never knew it had.

The men and women of World War II were many things—selfless, determined, humble, heroic—but they weren't immortal. Every day we lose a few more of the Greatest Generation. Every day we grow closer to a time when their stories will no longer be accompanied by a human pulse.

That sad fact has given urgency and passion to the fine book you hold in your hands. The men and women so lovingly captured here still have the spirit, the memories, the scars. They are living testimony. Their craggy faces hold great narratives of wisdom and pain. Their wistful expressions, their bittersweet smiles, speak volumes. For every line and liver-spot, for every hard-earned wrinkle, there is a story to tell. Their eyes—dimmed by age, clouded by cataracts—have seen things we can only imagine.

Whenever I think about the magnitude of the sacrifices made in World War II, I feel a kind of dull and awesome incomprehension. How could they have done and suffered so much—while complaining so little? I spent three extraordinary years interviewing veterans for *Ghost Soldiers*, a book about the 1945 Army Ranger rescue of five hundred Bataan Death March survivors. I went to their reunions, I traveled with them to the Philippines, I lingered with them in military cemeteries, where the long rows of white crucifixes went on and on, warping in the heat waves. The war was always playing in their heads—like ambient noise. They had slaved and starved. They'd seen friends tortured. They had buried legions of their comrades. They still woke up in the night, sweaty and scared, tormented by visions. Yet by and large, they wouldn't talk about it. They tended their memories in silence.

I became particularly fond of a Bataan veteran named Bert Bank, who lived in Tuscaloosa, Alabama. One afternoon when I was visiting him at his home, he decided to drive me over to Dreamland BBQ—Tuscaloosa's legendary pithouse. Riding with Bert proved one of the most terrifying experiences of my life. He was an absolutely atrocious driver. He kept turning into traffic, clipping curbs, tailgating, swerving. It took me awhile to figure out the problem: Bert was blind.

When he was a prisoner-of-war in the Philippines, vitamin deficiencies had robbed him of his sight. Over the decades, he'd regained some of his vision but he was still legally blind. Bert didn't want me to know this. It was a matter of pride and stoicism. He insisted on driving us. He had memorized the streets of Tuscaloosa; the route to Dreamland was hard-wired in his brain.

Somehow we got there in one piece—and the BBQ was magnificent. Afterward, though, I grabbed his keys and said: "Bert, I'm driving us home."

Bert passed away a few years ago. But his story illustrates something profound about so many of these veterans: Their resolve, their modesty, their quiet pride, their self-reliance, their refusal to complain. They don't think they did anything extraordinary. They don't want special treatment. They don't want to stand out at all.

Luckily for us, Thomas Sanders and Veronica Kavass had different ideas. They understood that these men and women do, and *should*, stand out—now more than ever. In creating this beautiful book, Sanders and Kavass have helped fulfill the most important responsibility a society bears toward those who served the nation in war: to pay homage.

Savor these powerful images and words, and take them as your cue. Seek out veterans close to you, talk to them, hear their stories. Understand what they accomplished. And appreciate the fact that history is living right in front of you.

— H.S., *Santa Fe, NM*

THE FACES OF HISTORY Thomas SANDERS

Randall HARRIS, Lieutenant, U.S. Army Rangers

THE FIRST WORLD WAR II VETERAN I PHOTOgraphed was Lt. Randall Harris. He showed me a six-inch scar on the bottom of his stomach. When I asked him how he'd gotten the large wound he told me this story. While stationed in Italy, his company's mission was to take the eastern half of the Sicilian town of Gela and form a perimeter. At the beginning of battle, his company commander triggered an S-mine and was killed instantly. S-mines are filled with steel balls which explode in a million directions when the mines are set off. Another S-mine exploded, and several of those steel balls hit Harris in his lower abdomen and legs. Randall took his canteen belt, tightened the strap around his wound and continued fighting.

That day he made it back to the aid station line at camp, and was waiting in a line of wounded soldiers. A medic was going through the line, to see who needed immediate attention, and when the medic came up to Randall, he was holding his intestines in with his hands. The medic tried to move Randall ahead of everyone, but he would not budge. "No one touches me, until all my men have been attended to," said Lt. Harris.

The year was 2006 when Randall told me his story. I was a twenty-one-year-old college senior at the time, stressing about my future as a photographer, my final exams, and the girl's phone number I was striving to get that weekend. When Randall was my age, his only goal was to live to the next day. I couldn't even fathom what that would feel like. Right then, I made a spontaneous decision. I was going to photograph and document as many World War II vets as I possibly could.

I began traveling up and down the California coast seeking out veterans. At first I was only photographing a few men and women a day, and then I received a commission from Belmont Village Senior Living Communities to visit their twenty prestigious locations around the country and photograph all the veterans living in their residences. It was a dream come true.

Following each visit, Belmont Village would unveil a permanent gallery of the photographs I'd taken to honor the vets. Each vet was individually recognized at an opening reception and received a print of their portrait. The events were deeply moving and uplifting for both the vets and the family members and loved ones that came to support them. Veterans who I'd had to beg to be photographed, slowly began to open up. They started pulling WWII memorabilia out of tucked away places in their rooms, they called me on the phone to share their recollections of the war, they began to take pride in being part of this book. I met vets who normally walked with walkers or wheel chairs, but would shove their walkers aside, or get up from their wheel chairs and stand with dignity and honor when I took their pictures. I met vets who had Alzheimer's who struggled tenaciously to tell me even a little bit about their war experience.

I hope when people see my images of the World War II veterans and read their stories, they become more appreciative of all those who have served our country and fought our wars. I hope when they are out in their communities and see a veteran or soldier, they go up to them, look them in their eyes, and tell them *thank you* for their sacrifices. It shouldn't matter if a soldier saw battle or not, if they were prepared to fight or fought. It shouldn't matter if they were in Germany, Korea, Vietnam, or Iraq. They have all made sacrifices for our safety and our future. As I heard from many of the vets, the soldier who does not return from war makes the ultimate sacrifice. My great uncle was in WWII and was torn in half by a mortar. I lost a great uncle, my grandpa lost a brother, my great grandma a son; and Bobby Sanders lost the chance of having a family, a career, and a full life.

Many of the veterans I photographed have passed away since we met. It is one of the most difficult parts of this project for me, but has also been a powerful reminder of why recording their images and memories is so urgently important. One day, very soon, they will not be here to tell their stories.

— T.S., *Los Angeles, CA*

THE VOICES OF HISTORY

Veronica KAVASS

I DID NOT EXPECT TO FIND VERY MUCH IN COMMON with the veterans I interviewed for this book. They represent a time of unflinching patriotism and spiffy uniforms. They understood the importance of following orders and keeping secrets. From where I am standing, so much of this has changed today. We seem to uphold different values now—transparency of information, political correctness and comfortable, if not, sloppy attire. As a country, we are incredibly divided on every major issue. Picking sides can be a hassle, there is an increasing propensity to ignore the issues all together. Such behavior would have been unheard of during the Second World War.

I am a young woman with an endless penchant for stories. This was the main draw to this project: I knew it would be a story gold mine. As I listened to each veteran share his or her memories, I realized I had something in common with all of them, namely, a curiosity to see the world. Most of them were very young—*too young*—when they enlisted. Charles Hill enlisted in 1940 "at the ripe old age of 15" because it was "the only way for a country boy to see the world." When all of his peers were impatiently waiting to get back home, John Jackson stuck around Europe after the war ended to study languages and international law. There are numerous accounts of veterans who looked at military enlistment as their only opportunity to travel. I know what it is like to be young and eager to see what's beyond the cow fence. I also went overseas at the age of eighteen—I was armed with a small guitar, a Spanish dictionary, and hiking boots. Of course, I saw the world through a very different filter.

After twenty interviews I began tracing patterns. There were a surprising number of plane crash survivors. Poor eyesight prohibiting entrance into the Navy or Air Force was another very common pattern. I heard echoes: "You aren't scared of death when you are eighteen." Along with, "Anyone who said they weren't scared, was lying." Nearly everyone I interviewed was proud to serve in the war. A majority considered our current war a complete mess. One thing I know about storytelling is that there is a tendency to leave out the parts we don't understand. But when someone decides to come face-to-face with it while telling the story, it always enriches the narration. Like when Sumner Glimcher explained why he could no longer shoot his rifle after seeing his first dead American soldier. It is hard to admit to being a soldier who pretended to pull the trigger, but he did, and it made his story stronger.

While I found myself relating to many of the thoughts and emotions during our conversations, I struggled with certain issues when it came to editing their stories. For example, certain terms that are considered racial epithets today—such as referring to the Japanese as "Japs." To this day it is natural for World War II veterans to use that term. And why not? Major American newspapers repeatedly put it in their headlines during the course of the war. Official awards

"The ones that really sacrificed aren't here to answer. The rest of us have to speak for them."

— **Milton HOLMEN**

and commendations would state, "Congratulations for beating the Japs!" It was an acceptable term then. Now it isn't. What is my duty in this? To maintain authenticity or change it out of respect? This was a pickle. Perhaps the answer lies in the fact that I was too timid to ask the three Japanese-American veterans I interviewed what they thought of this conundrum.

The biggest challenge with this assignment was the race with time. These stories are slipping away and I didn't really take that into account until I found myself chasing after them. We wanted to cover every aspect of World War II, but that wasn't a simple process. I was given a list of the veterans Tom Sanders had photographed in the past four years. A number of them had already passed on and many others could no longer remember that far back. That's why it was incredible to get a story from Edna Davis, one of the last three hundred WASP aviators left in the world. Or Harold Mason who was in the only topographic engineering company in the European Theater. Sanders even tracked down connecting stories between a POW survivor, Morton Gollins, and a soldier, Tom Gibbons, who was in the first squadron that liberated his camp, Stalag Luft VIIA. It was Gibbons, a natural raconteur, who ended his story with, "The most important thing to remember about this was: The true heroes are the ones who never came home." In the pause that followed that statement, I could feel the resounding absence of all those stories.

— V.K., *New York City, NY*

Milton HOLMEN, Captain, U.S. Army Medical Service Corps

"The next morning I was shaving when the radio announced, 'This is the Real McCoy! Pearl Harbor's being bombed!'"

— AL GETTER

I WORKED AS A CIVILIAN RIGGER IN Pearl Harbor and was supposed to be at work that Sunday but had passed my shift off. I wanted to go on a date and knew one of my coworkers was married with kids. He took my overtime happily, and that night I went to see some bullfighting movie called *Blood and Sand*. The next morning I was shaving when the radio announced, "This is the Real McCoy! Pearl Harbor's being bombed!" I caught a ride down to Pearl Harbor and found two destroyers lying one on top of the other. The old southern quartermaster, "Turkey Neck" Thompson, was shouting at a group of men holding hoses. When he saw me he said, "Grab on to that hose!" We were fighting fire. There were three ships in the dry dock, including the battleship *Pennsylvania*. The two ships in front of the Pennsylvania were the *Cassin* and the *Downes*, and they were hit much harder than the Penny.[1] As soon as I picked up a hose, I had to drop it and dive into a concrete block toilet. A Japanese plane was making another round, peppering with his machine gun, and I lay down alongside the toilets with my eyes shut until he finished playing. I was angry as hell.

I was ordered to check on the Marine Corps, where I found skip boxes being loaded with the dead and wounded. The dead were placed out on the lawn, and the wounded were sent to the hospital. I helped unload. Everything moved very quickly, and sometimes my hands were unsteady as I shifted bodies. I accidentally ended up riding with the wounded to the hospital, leaving the rows of corpses behind. On his way back, the hospital truck dropped me off at my regular post, the rope locker, in time to witness it catch on fire. A sixty-five-year-old Scotsman named Ferguson put the fire out and, consequently, saved the ships' blueprints. That was wise, because once they started bringing in the injured ships, we knew how to fix them.

I wanted to go back to sea because that's where I belonged. They sent me back to the mainland on a Liberty ship.[2] I went to officers school in Alameda, CA, graduated, and shipped out to sea again with the merchant marine.[3] We had a lot of 4Fs on board—the ones the military turned down for failing their physicals.[4] We didn't care. We took men with heart conditions, poor eyesight, limps. "Hey, you want to go? Are you sixteen years old? Yeah, okay, come aboard." Our skipper was nearly seventy—there was no age limit on board.

We left San Pedro with a cargo of ammunition and miscellaneous supplies. It was our job to supply the Navy, Army, and Marine Corps with everything they needed for the invasions. After stopping in Australia to pick up food and supplies, our ship almost ended up in Antarctica. It was tricky to navigate around all the Japanese subs off the coast of Australia; we weren't equipped well enough to see what was around us. Late one night, when we were nearing Calcutta, the captain called me up and asked, "You know how to recognize Navy ships?" I nodded. He pointed out and said, "What are those ships?" I took the binoculars and looked out. "Captain, they're not U.S." He asked, "Are they Japanese?" "I don't know!" When daylight came, we found ourselves smack in the middle of a fleet of British war ships. I asked the gunnery officer, "What in the hell would you do if we found out that we were in the

Al Getter, early 1930s.

Lieutenant Commander, U.S. Maritime Service[5]

Getter (far right) and crew of the President Hoover in 1936.

middle of a Japanese fleet?" He told me we would have fought, of course. "Fight? With what?"

For our last trip, we loaded thousands of barrels of fog oil onboard and attached ourselves to the Seventh Fleet for the big Japanese invasion. However, that nasty little thing called the atomic bomb was dropped. Afterward, the Japanese told General MacArthur, "Well, you've conquered us, so feed us." They didn't have anything. They fought until they were just nothing left. MacArthur brought us up there and told them, "You can have this oil. Go fishing." So we unloaded five or six thousand barrels, and this Japanese guy helping me said, "You're five barrels short." I think he was joking, but I told him to scram. Several days later, he asked, "How long a time before we friends again?" I told him, "About twenty years." He exclaimed, "Why so long?" I said, "Because you just sneak-bombed us." And he said, "Must do! Japan little country!" He squatted down to demonstrate. Then he stood up, spread his arms, and smiled. "America *big* country!"

1 The USS *Pennsylvania* was the flagship of the United States Fleet. During the attack on Pearl Harbor, *Pennsylvania* was in dry dock with the USS *Cassin* and the USS *Downes*. An incendiary bomb exploded between *Cassin* and *Downes*, causing severe damage to both. *Pennsylvania* escaped with relatively light damage, and was repaired and returned to service in 1942. Both *Cassin* and *Downes* were salvaged and also joined the war.

2 Built by welding (rather than riveting) prefabricated sections together, Liberty ships were relatively inexpensive and easy to manufacture, and played an important role as cargo ships during World War II.

3 The United States Merchant Marine is the commercial fleet of ships involved in the maritime trade and transport of goods and materials. The Merchant Marine Act of 1936 made the fleet auxiliary to the U.S. Navy in times of war, and in 1988 President Ronald Reagan signed legislation granting veteran status to mariners who served in war.

4 A rating of the military conscription service, 4F indicated a person unfit for service under the established physical, mental, or moral standards of the U.S. military.

5 The United States Maritime Service was established in 1938 with the purpose of developing the existing merchant marine force into an efficient and well-trained work force able to promote commerce and aid in national defense. The program employed civilian and U.S. Coast Guard instructors, and followed Coast Guard rank structure.

"I spent most of my time in basic training, helping to train new recruits. I turned boys into men."

William KING, Seaman, U.S. Navy

The Raft

Opposite: **John MAY, Seaman Third Class, U.S. Navy** Above: **George KARAGEORGE, Crew Chief, U.S. Army Air Corps**

THEY DRAFTED ME TWO DAYS BEFORE Pearl Harbor, but I was sent home because my heart was wrong. My *this* was wrong, my *that* was wrong; everything was wrong. That was on a Friday. On Sunday, Pearl Harbor happened. Monday morning, the Army calls me back again. "We have to reexamine you." And what do you know? I turned into the healthiest guy in the world. They put me in a cab with a couple of other boys and took me to the O'Hare airfield in Chicago. Eight hours later, I was in Hawaii.

They told me I was in the Seventh Air Force. Sounded good to me. I met with the captain and he asked, "So you're a pretty good mechanic?" "Yeah, yeah," I told him. I *lied*. My papers said I worked for Blue Star Auto in Chicago for three years. When they assigned me to aircraft mechanics, I started getting nervous. I didn't actually know how to fix planes—it just sounded like a swell gig. When you start telling lies, you spend your whole life trying to get from one lie to the other.

The next day I met with my newly assigned captain in his office. I asked him if I could make a statement. "Captain," I said, "everything you see on that record is a lot of BS. I only worked for Blue Star for about three weeks." He looked at me for a while—the way teachers have looked at me certain times in my life—and said, "Well, what do you want to do?" I told him, "Here I am, you're examining me, I'm telling you the truth. I don't know the front end from the back end on an airplane."

The Captain sighed but looked a little amused. "Okay, at least you're honest," he said. "Now I'll tell you what I want you to do—I want you to meet the boy who is the head of the maintenance department. Now he's an old veteran and he's ready to leave. He was supposed to be discharged. He married a Hawaiian girl and has a whole family. He'll stay with you about a month, teach you as much as he can get into your head, and then he's going." I was ecstatic. He wagged his finger at me, "Don't BS these guys." I spent four or five months there, and then we were sent down to a little island called Kanton in the South Pacific. It was as big as a postage stamp. All white. No dirt. No trees. Just plain white sand.

Sergeant, U.S. Air Force

We were in the 333d Squadron by this point. We hopped from island to island, following the Marines as they knocked them out to get to the Japanese. I was in the Air Force, attached to the Navy, and assigned to the Marines. I was nothing! My officer would tell me, "Fred, you're going to get all kinds of garbage. God willing, you're going to end up with forty airplanes, and I want to have the maximum of forty airplanes ready to fly. Beg. Borrow. Steal. Except one thing: if I ask you what happened, I want the truth so I know how to cover for you."

Some days were calm and we had fun. And there were some days when the Japs attacked us. We would get into a foxhole until it was over. We'd push our way out of the sand and find a blown-off arm. There was always damage. People always got hit. So we had to have regular burials. They used to take the boys—all the pieces of the parts of their bodies—out to the far end of the island, whichever island we happened to be on, and dig a deep hole, and dump everyone in it like garbage. Closed it up and that was it.

"A simple question was periodically asked: 'Are you willing to serve wherever ordered?' Any that answered 'Yes' were cleared and transferred to the 442nd, the MIS, or the Panama Canal. When the war ended, there remained one hundred and twenty of us who continued to answer 'No.'"

— **Cedrick SHIMO**

Cedrick Shimo (center) with fellow soldiers at Camp Grant, Illinois.

Cedrick SHIMO

Private, U.S. Army

ON DECEMBER 7TH, 1941, I WAS A graduate student at University of California at Berkeley. The very next day I received my draft notice from the Los Angeles draft board. When I arrived at the train depot with my notice in hand, I was refused passage because I looked like the enemy. They feared I would sabotage their train. That was the first time I was referred to as a "dirty Jap." I had no choice but to hitchhike to Los Angeles and subsequently to Illinois for basic training.

While I was in Illinois, my dad was arrested by the FBI. He was imprisoned along with thousands of other *Issei*—Buddhist priests, community leaders, teachers, martial arts instructors, and businessmen.[1] My dad was arrested because he operated a kendo fencing school. Judo, kendo, karate, and other martial arts activities belonged to an association in Japan called Butoku Kai. The U.S. government erroneously connected Butoku Kai with Kokuryūkai—the Black Dragon Association—which was an ultra-nationalistic group.[2]

After Pearl Harbor, most of the *Nisei* serving in the Army were transferred to concentration camps.[3] They were classified as 4-C, enemy aliens, and considered unsuitable for military service. A majority of the five thousand *Nisei* already serving in the army were discharged.

A Military Intelligence school was established in Camp Savage in Minnesota.[4] I volunteered to be in the MIS in late December 1942 and was transferred to Camp Savage by January.

As the news about our families started to trickle in, many heated discussions were held at our barracks. My parents were confined to different camps—my father was held by the Department of Justice, but my mother was held in Manzanar, which was run by the War Relocation Authority.[5] They were not obligated to abide by the Geneva Convention, and we heard tales of severe brutality and even killings by the guards. Why had we volunteered for this assignment when our families were being mistreated by the very same government we were serving?

Despite our grumbling, we continued to study hard. Most of the students in my class were *Kibei*, and I had to work twice as hard just to keep up.[6] I remember studying in the latrine when the barracks' lights were turned out.

Just prior to graduating, we all applied for a two-week furlough. I requested a visit to Manzanar to bid farewell to my mother before shipping out to the Pacific front. My application was turned down because at that early point in the war, no Japanese Americans, not even soldiers, were allowed on the West Coast. I complained bitterly and was suddenly expelled from school.

In fact, twenty of us were ejected from the school—not as a single group, but in pairs. Kenichi Ichinose and I were sent to Fort Leavenworth—a plush pre-war Army camp. No barracks, but comfortable sturdy brick buildings that sat on tree-lined streets. There was a fishing pond, a swimming pool, and an athletic field where we played baseball. I worked as a clerk in the motor pool. These were utterly confusing times.

Months later, we were transferred to Fort Leonard Wood, Missouri. I was placed with *Nisei* malcontents from various Army camps, along with American soldiers of German and Italian descent. All considered potential troublemakers, we were demoted to the lowest possible rank and placed in a "do nothing" unit formed just for the purpose of keeping us all under one roof for observation. Our meaningless daily tasks were the equivalent of digging a hole and then refilling it.

Since I was able to type, I was later reassigned from pick-and-shovel duty to operating a dog-tag machine—punching metal dog tags eight hours a day. It was a boring job, but I entertained myself by sending Christmas greetings and other messages on the dog tags.

To help ease the manpower shortage during the war, a decision was made for us to contribute to the war effort by putting us to work. Our unit was reorganized as the 1800th Engineers and shipped to various Southern states, such as Mississippi, Louisiana, and Arkansas. Our duty was to follow combat troops on training maneuvers and to repair the damage to roads, fences, and bridges caused by heavy tanks and heavy-duty trucks. We were a full-fledged engineering battalion with all the necessary equipment. We had everything except for weapons.

A simple question was periodically asked: "Are you willing to serve wherever ordered?" Any that answered "Yes" were cleared and transferred to the 442nd, the MIS, or the Panama Canal. When the war ended, there remained one hundred and twenty of us who continued to answer "No."

I was once interviewed by a government intelligence officer who asked, "If Japan invaded the United States and was approaching the camps, which side would you fight for?" I told him I would fight for whichever side was defending the camps. Everything I held dear in my life was in the camps. I asked him, "Would the guards defend our camps or would they be machine-gunning the inmates? Would they prevent American civilians from entering the camps and slaughtering my friends and family?" Neither of us had the answer.

Military portrait of Cedrick Shimo.

---

1 *Issei* is a Japanese language term for Japanese immigrants, particularly to the United States. Their children, born in the adoptive country, are known as *Nisei*. The terms are formed by combining the Japanese number that corresponds to the generation (*ichi*; *ni*) with the word for generation (*sei*).

2 Kokuryūkai, or the Black Dragon Society, was an extremist Japanese organization formed in 1901 to drive Russia out of East Asia. Their efforts included covert intelligence and espionage training, and by the 1930s it had developed into a right-wing political organization with a fiercely nationalist platform, and included prominent members of business, government, and the military.

3 See footnote 1.

4 Camp Savage, located in the town of Savage, Minnesota, was the primary location of a language school operated by the United States' Military Intelligence Service (MIS). The school recruited Japanese Americans from the military and internment camps to teach American soldiers the Japanese language.

5 The War Relocation Authority was an agency created in 1942 to oversee the internment of Americans of Japanese, German, and Italian descent. It organized the removal of approximately one hundred and twenty thousand people, primarily Japanese Americans, to ten camps situated in the western United States. Manzanar was located in Owens Valley, California, and was the first camp created in the aftermath of Pearl Harbor, and held over ten thousand prisoners during its operation.

6 *Kibei* is a Japanese language term for second-generation Japanese Americans. They differ from *Nisei* in that, while having been born in America, they traveled to Japan to receive a formal education before returning to the States.

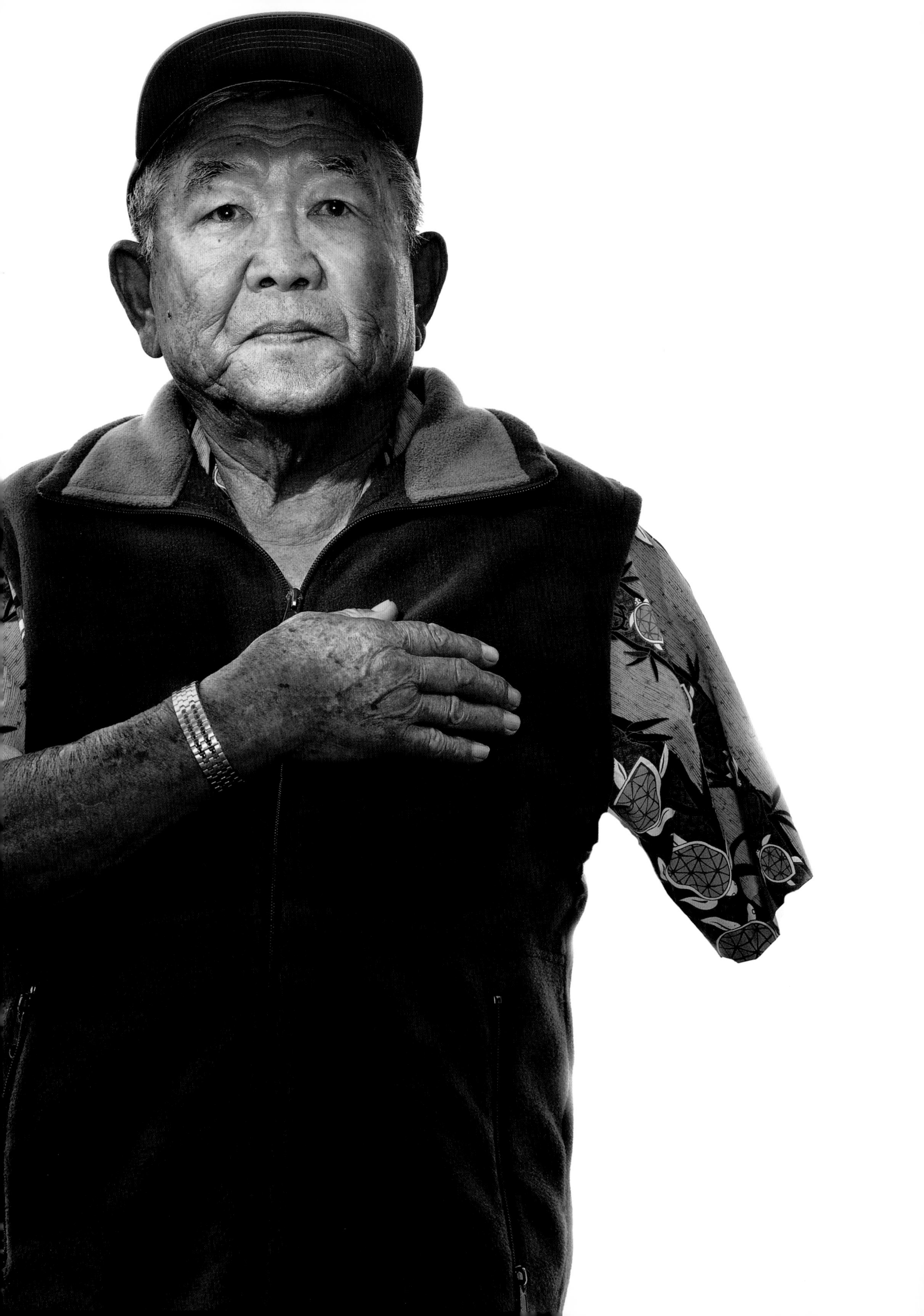

Don SEKI

Corporal, U.S. Army

I WAS BORN IN OAHU, HAWAII, during the Depression. We lived in the middle of a cane field in Waipahu. There was nobody to talk to or play with except my family. I graduated high school in June 1941, and that October, my parents decided to return to Japan. I wanted no part of Japan and remained behind by myself. Japanese custom is strict, and it was a big step to disobey my parents.

On December 6th, a group of us were playing poker at our teacher's house. All of a sudden, from nowhere, three Filipino laborers came up to the house and shouted, "You bomb Pearl Harbor!" And I said, "What? I'm right here. Pearl Harbor's right over there."

War broke out, and so did curfew and military police. I was mad at the Japanese. They instantly became my enemy. We were Americans. I believed you did anything for your country, whether you had to die or not. That was a Japanese motto. If the Japanese had invaded Oahu, we *Nisei* would have fought them.[1] But nothing happened to Hawaii after Pearl Harbor, and we were barred from being in the armed forces. Eventually, in 1943, they told us, "You're American now, you can volunteer." Ten thousand *Nisei* volunteered. They shipped three thousand of us from Honolulu to California. From there we traveled to Mississippi. They had never seen our kind of people down south. When our commanding officer met us, he said, "You are not white. You are not black. But you are American!" And we proudly said, "Yes, we are!" But in downtown Hattiesburg, about twenty-five miles out of Camp Shelby, we were a problem.[2] The local white people didn't want us there.

I saw how they treated the Negro people—like dirt! We couldn't understand that, and we didn't like it. So we went to the black restaurant. Some of the whites told us not to go, but we said, "We can go anywhere we want." If one guy from our group got in trouble—ohhh boy. Everybody helped out. We never damaged property, but we used to fight them. We had a motto: "Go for broke!"

I was in the 442nd Infantry.[3] We had just retaken Bruyères from the Germans when they told us that the 36th Division had been surrounded by Germans in the Vosges forest and were trapped. They asked my battalion to rescue them. The 3rd Battalion consisted of four companies, and they sent two: Companies I and K. Each company had about 180 men. When it was over, there were only twenty-five men left. The rest were injured or dead. My company was fully intact, because we'd been held in reserve. We were sent in as a "mop-up" group. On November 4th, I got hit by machine gun fire that took my arm off. Just dangling skin left. That was the end of combat for me.

I was sent to an orthopedic hospital in Brigham City, Utah. It was mainly amputees, paraplegics, and paralyzed patients. We had to go through occupational and physical therapy. They gave me a temporary artificial limb and I had to learn how to hold a fork with it. I also had to go horseback riding, and hold the reign with my artificial limb. They even got us fishing reels and we fished for trout. We took the fish to the local restaurant, and those beautiful people fried it up and gave us beer.

When I got discharged around Christmas of 1946, I decided to go see my folks. The only way I could get to Japan was if I worked for the military or the federal government. I took a job as a federal employee in 1947 and eventually made it onto a propeller plane heading to Japan. From Tokyo station, I caught a locomotive train—no bullet train then—and six hours later I arrived in Fukushima. When my parents saw me, they almost wept. They said, "One wing?" And I told them, "It's okay. I'm alive. I came home."

---

1 *Nisei* is a Japanese language term for children born to Japanese immigrants in a new country. The word is formed by combining the Japanese number that corresponds to the generation (*ni*) with the Japanese word for generation (*sei*).

2 Camp Shelby, located in southern Mississippi, was established in 1917 as a basic training facility. It expanded vastly during World War II, ultimately offering one thousand acres of training space and hosting a convalescent hospital and prisoner-of-war camp on the grounds.

3 The 442nd Regimental Combat Team (now Infantry) was a mostly Japanese American unit that fought in the European Theater during World War II, and would go on to become the most highly decorated regiment in the history of the U.S. military. One of the unit's most famous—and costly—victories came during the rescue of the 141st Infantry Regiment, a battalion attached to the 36th Division that had been surrounded by German forces in the Vosges region of France. After two previous unsuccessful rescue attempts, the 442nd were tasked with breaking through and rescuing the so-called "Lost Battalion." After five days of fighting, on October 30, 1944, they succeeded, despite suffering over eight hundred casualties, including 121 dead.

"Six planes hit our ship. We lost forty men in about fifty minutes. But they just couldn't sink the ship. So we had the privilege of saying that we got hit with more kamikaze planes during World War II than any other ship and didn't sink."

— Carl E. CLARK

Carl E. CLARK

I WAS AN ORPHAN. MY PARENTS DIED and there were five of us kids. We were scattered all over the country, and I lived with some people in the Colorado countryside. I was the only black kid in the whole school. I got along fine. And in fact, the teachers and the faculty, they spoiled me because they let me get away with things they wouldn't let other people get away with. I was in the harmonica band—oh, I did everything! When they would have their birthday parties, I was always invited.

It was 1936 and the Great Depression was going on. People were starving in the streets. So anything was better than nothing. When I joined the Navy, I wasn't prepared for the racism I encountered. I'd have officers tell me, "We've looked at your record, and you act different than these other boys." Now, what he meant by that was—most of the black crew were from the deep, deep South. And that's when that deep, deep segregation and prejudice was going on. And they'd been brought up with all of that. Their parents had taught them: "Make sure you don't make that white man mad," and "Don't sass that white man, don't look that white man in the face when you talk to him." I didn't know anything about that. I would look an officer in the eye and talk to him, and I would act just like I did when I was in Colorado. And a lot of those officers didn't like that. They didn't want to have somebody putting the idea in these black men's heads that they could be like white people. They wanted them to stay just like those people they got from down in the deep South, and say "Yes, suh" and grin and all that kind of stuff. But they couldn't change me. So I caught hell. But I did move on up as high I could go in the Navy.

I was stationed at a brand new base in Kaneohe Bay, Hawaii.[1] Pearl Harbor was right across the island from us. On the morning of December 7th, I had what they called "the duty," which meant I had to wake up the officers. It was Sunday, and too early to wake them, so I was sitting there in a room when the planes flew over, strafing. A bullet came through my window, bounced around, and just missed me and landed in one of the chairs. I ran around and woke up the officers, told them what was going on. The planes burned up all of our brand new PBY seaplanes.[2] They had to circle two or three times to get them all. We didn't have any guns, we didn't have anything. We just watched the show—just like it was a movie or something.

A year after, they put me on the *Aaron Ward*—a Navy destroyer.[3] I was twenty-seven years old, and at that time they were having a hard time getting enough draftees, so most of the crew were young kids—eighteen, nineteen years old. The older sailors taught the young men the various jobs. It took about six months. Then down to the South Pacific to get into the fight. During the invasion of Okinawa, our job was to shoot down all the enemy aircraft.[4] The Japanese had just lost the air war, and now they were using their planes as missiles. They would load them with bombs and gas and fly their planes directly into the ship; nothing but bombs. Six planes hit our ship. We lost forty men in about fifty minutes. They killed a whole lot of men, but they just couldn't sink the ship. So we had the privilege of saying that we got hit with more kamikaze planes during World War II than any other ship and didn't sink. I got wounded that day while I was putting out fires on the ship. I wasn't the only man. Somebody was there helping me a little bit on the hose, because we only had one hose that was operational, and it usually took two men to operate it. But there were times when I was on that hose there by myself. In the end, the ship was mangled. It was nothing but a junkyard.

The next morning, the captain of the ship found me sitting on the deck—everybody was kind of in a daze. I started to get up when I saw him approaching me. He said, "No, no, don't get up." So I stayed where I was. He crouched down in front of me, and he said, "I want to thank you because you saved my ship."

Chief Petty Officer, U.S. Navy

Carl Clark with his wife, Florence, 1944.

But when they got together and decided who was going to get a medal, they weren't going to give me one. All the prejudice that was going on at the time, I can understand why. There were three hundred men aboard that ship. Only six of them were black men. So here we got only six black men aboard the ship, and one of them the captain credits for saving it—that would have been pretty embarrassing for the captain, and for the Navy.

After that, nobody said anything to me about it, and I didn't say anything either. I thought it was all forgotten. About ten years ago, my son was looking in a military magazine and he saw the name of the ship. We did a little investigation, and I found that one of the officers from the ship lived about thirty-five miles from me. So I found him, and we talked. He asked me to come up and address his club—about two hundred people. And when he introduced me, he introduced me as the man that the captain said saved his ship. And that's the first time that I'd ever heard that.

Right now, one of my congressmen is trying to get me some kind of recognition for what I did. There was a lot of terrible prejudice going on during those times—you see, us few black men on that ship, the white officers certainly didn't like us. I went to one of the reunions, and those same sailors—they acted the same way toward me. The only people that associated with me at the reunion were some of those guys' daughters and sons, and a few of their wives. They didn't realize that if it hadn't been for me, a lot of them probably wouldn't have even been there.

I've talked about my story to many different groups. And every time, that's the first question they ask me: "How did you stand it?" The thing was, when you are around that kind of pressure all the time, you don't like it, but you get used to the pressure. At the time, I couldn't do anything about it. I really didn't have any hatred about it. Most of the time, I just thought it was their ignorance.

I retired at the highest rate that a black man could get in those days, as a chief petty officer. And when I was on an aircraft carrier, I slept in a chief petty officer's quarters. Now, I can remember a time when black men could not sleep in the same compartment with a white man, no matter what he was. I'm ninety-three now. We have a black president. We have black congressmen. We have black senators. I knew the situation would change, but I didn't think it would change this much in my lifetime.

---

1 Naval Air Station Kaneohe Bay was a seaplane base commissioned on February 15th, 1941. On December 7th, 1941, Japanese aircraft attacked the base several minutes before the attack on Pearl Harbor, destroying the majority of the American aircraft there.

2 Introduced in 1936, the PBY Catalina was an American seaplane used during World War II for patrol, search-and-rescue, and anti-submarine missions. The P and B in the name stood for Patrol Boat, with the Y indicating its manufacturer, Consolidated Aircraft.

3 The third USS *Aaron Ward* was commissioned by the U.S. Navy on October 28th, 1944. A destroyer, she operated in the Pacific as a minelayer, participating in the Okinawa invasion. On May 3rd, 1945, she endured several attacks by Japanese kamikaze planes, but kept from sinking. Upon completing repairs, the *Aaron Ward* returned to the States, but was ultimately decommissioned in September 1945 due to the extent of the damage she sustained.

4 The Battle of Okinawa was the last major battle of the Pacific War. The largest Allied amphibious assault, it lasted from April to June 1945, with the objective of securing a base of operations within striking distance of mainland Japan. It resulted in one of the highest casualty rates of any World War II conflict, with more than one hundred thousand Japanese and fifty thousand Allied casualties, as well as more than one hundred thousand civilian casualties.

Above: **Eugene WASHINGTON, Steward Second Class, U.S. Navy** Opposite: **William F. SMITH, Seaman First Class, U.S. Navy**

4
14
U.S

I ENLISTED IN 1940 AT THE RIPE OLD age of fifteen years old. I didn't think it was too young. I felt ten feet tall. Besides, there was no war then. That was the only way for a country boy to see the world. I wanted to go to Hawaii, but the recruiting sergeant and my father talked me into going to Fort Knox, Kentucky, which was twenty-five miles from my home. They told me that I could take a short discharge and go to Hawaii in a year. I took their advice, but I never did get to Hawaii, thank goodness. I wound up in the European Theater fighting Adolf.

I went over in February of 1944 and stayed in England until D-Day. My outfit, the 704th Tank Destroyer Battalion, entered France two weeks later. We were what they called a "bastard outfit"—we didn't have a father. We were constantly assigned to different units that needed our firepower.

The vehicle that we drove was built like a tank, only it wasn't one—it was a tank destroyer called the Hellcat.[1] It's much lighter than a tank, and therefore much faster. Tanks drove at about twenty-five miles an hour, and we could run sixty. We traveled forty and fifty miles a day. We didn't do city fighting, we fought out in the open. Our tank was made to hit and run, and when German tanks came in to view, we'd shoot them and then we'd hide again. We had a 76mm gun that would knock out almost any German tank, with the exception of a Tiger tank.[2] And we still knocked out a few of those!

There were some scary experiences. Little incidents come to my mind—be it one day or one hour in a battle, I never forget the times when I should have gotten killed. One of them was at Arracourt.[3] I had been the assistant driver in the lead tank, but I didn't get along with the driver so I traded with the guy in the second tank. After we switched, the lead tank blew up. Or the time when I realized we drove the tank halfway across the continent and I had never checked the oil in my torque converter. I was beating myself up for forgetting to do that, and I dropped my seat down to check the oil. About the moment I hit the bottom, a big gun fired a round of high-explosive ammunition that hit several yards in front of my tank. When I came back up to see what had happened, there was a piece of shrapnel sticking out of the leather where I had rested my head. I stared at it for a long time, because that shrapnel would have been in the middle of my head if I hadn't checked the oil.

We were always on the line, no time for leave—just go, go, go! You got to know the men in your tank pretty well. We were like five brothers. You had to get along, you had no place else to go. One time we were able to settle into a quiet German village for six days. I knew that some crews forced civilians to move out of their houses, but my crew would never make the people leave. We told them we were going to stay in their homes and they had the option to leave. They always stuck around.

This house we moved into, the lady was very belligerent when we first arrived, and she told us that we could not stay in her house. She said, "Well, my husband is an SS officer, and if he were here, you couldn't stay!" So we told her, "Well, lady, if your husband were here, he would either be dead or in a prison someplace." That kind of cooled her down a little bit. She finally wound up cooking meals for us—even flashed a smile now and then. She realized we were just kids away from home.

Several months after the war was over, they discharged me and sent me home; they didn't have any more use for me. I had joined the Army to see the world, and I can't say the war was what I had in mind when I was fifteen. I visited with my family in Louisville and went to Texas to get married—and started another war.

---

1 Nicknamed the Hellcat, the M18 Gun Motor Carriage was designed for speed and mobility. Lightweight and powerful, it was deployed primarily in Western Europe, and its function as a tank destroyer played a key role in various offensives.

2 "Tiger" was the nickname of two classes of heavy German tanks, the Panzerkampfwagen VI Ausführung H, and the Panzerkampfwagen Tiger Ausführung B. Both models carried very thick armor and heavy firepower at the expense of mobility and speed.

3 The town of Arracourt, France, was the site of intense fighting between U.S. and German armored forces in September 1944.

Corporal, U.S. Army

I DIDN'T PLAN ON SERVING IN THE military. I was pulled out of Roosevelt's fish bowl in the first draft. I went in the same day as Jimmy Stewart. He came down in a big bus full of photographers. Of course, I didn't have any photographers.

Two years after Pearl Harbor, we were deployed to Europe. We went over the ocean in January. Colder than the devil—ocean's rough that time of the year. They put us in what they called "the coffin corner," the ship they figured would be first to get hit by a torpedo.[1] We made a rest stop along the way when we were heading around the Brest peninsula. There was kind of a ditch where I decided to settle for the night. Suddenly I realized I was sitting next to a man in a German uniform. I just froze. I didn't know if he was alive or not. After a few minutes I checked him over to make sure he wasn't breathing and noticed he was smelling a little, too. It put chills through me—that was the first German I'd seen.

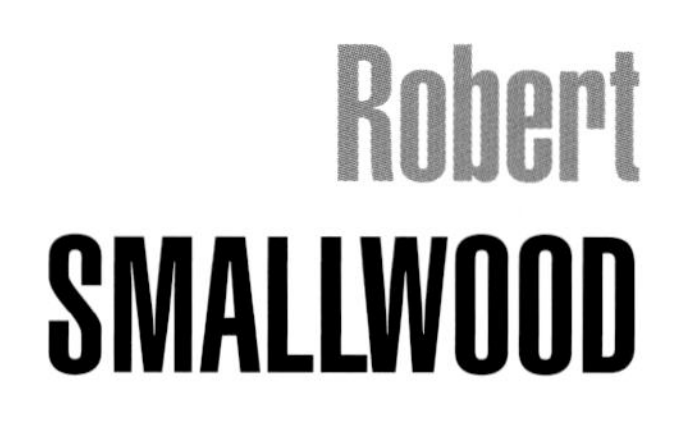

Smallwood in uniform, 1942.

I always felt sorry for anybody who got knocked off. The German army was making fifteen- and sixteen-year-old kids fight. If I came across those kids, I treated them real good and I sent them back to the American MPs. But when we got a Gestapo agent or SS guy, we'd take them down to the French MPs. I knew what they were doin' with them. The French hated their guts. That's where I sent those SS boys.[2]

Five days before the war was over, three of us got a truck and went up to Berchtesgaden, where Hitler's home was.[3] We wanted to see it. It was bombed, but not completely destroyed. There was a room that looked like it might be the master bedroom, and there was a key sticking in the door. So I just took it out and put it in my pocket. The room had big, beautiful gold drapes. I used my knife to cut a couple of tassels off, and put them in my pocket, too. Those were my souvenirs.

They made provisional MPs out of us. My buddy and I were assigned to the brothel, and we were supposed to keep the GIs from going in there, for health reasons. We had an awful time, because the airborne divisions were in town, and they were tough boys. Those guys would climb through the windows to get in. Well, we didn't try to stop them, as long as they didn't go through the front door. I made an exchange with the gal that ran it. See, I'd taken a lot of prisoners from Normandy all the way to Salzburg, and they used to trade me money for things. So I had quite a bundle. After the war was over, they issued invasion money for us to use. It was just like our money over here. This gal that ran the house, she didn't like these guys giving her invasion money, so I traded her German money for the invasion money, which was over fifteen hundred dollars. I went right to the post office and sent it home to my wife. That money was the first down payment on our house in 1945.

I was hoping we'd come into New York Harbor and see the Statue of Liberty. But no, we went into Boston. Still, they gave us a really good welcome. All the fireboats were out in the water, foghorns going. When I came back, my two-year-old son, he didn't want me to get in bed with his mother! He was throwing a fit. He didn't know me, but we became best buddies real quick.

Corporal, U.S. Army

1 The term "coffin corner" is used in a variety of circumstances, including aviation terminology and as the nickname of an October 1942 battle in the South Pacific. Use of the term in a marine context refers to the positioning of ships in a convoy: the coffin corner is the last ship of a line or row, the one most exposed to attack.

2 The Schutzstaffel (SS), or "protective squadron," was a Nazi paramilitary organization that was fiercely loyal to Hitler and Nazi ideology. Under the command of Nazi party leader and military commander Heinrich Himmler, the SS was responsible for numerous war crimes, including much of the organizing and implementation of the Holocaust.

3 Located in the Bavarian Alps, the town of Berchtesgaden sat underneath the mountain retreat of Obersalzberg, a popular vacation area. After being elected Chancellor of Germany in 1933, Adolf Hitler bought and expanded a chalet there, naming it Berghof. The Berghof was bombed and burned before eventually being stripped by Allied forces at the end of the war.

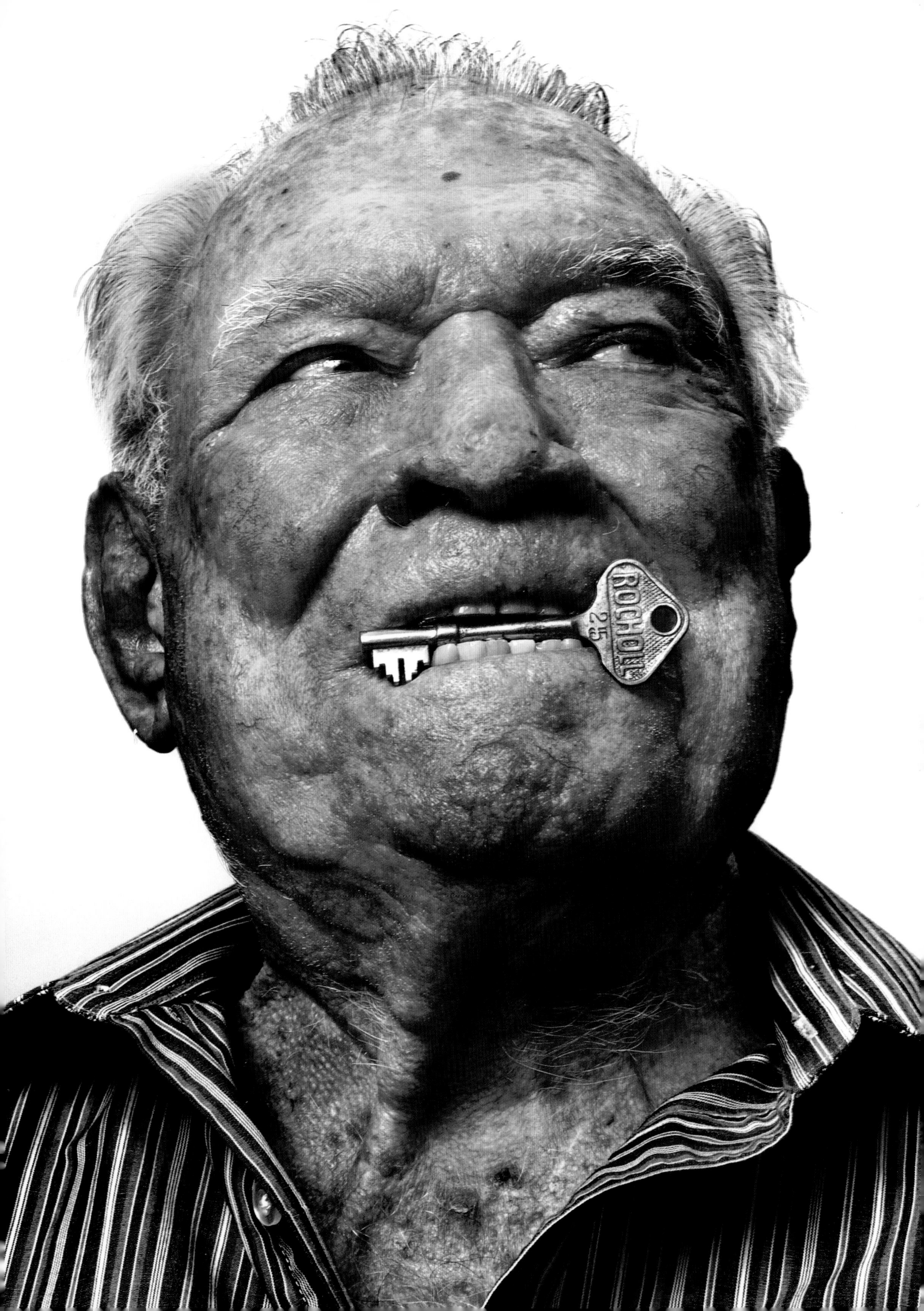
ROCHOLL
25

Above: **John POPEJOY, Lieutenant Colonel, U.S. Army Reserve** Opposite: **Edward R. GAUL, Second Lieutenant, U.S. Army Signal Corps**
Following spread: **Donald DENEEN, Seaman, U.S. Navy; Ray HAM, Engineer Third Class, U.S. Navy**

U.S.
W1DEF
W1JNC
ITALY
XACB
W4IIX

To Mother and Dad—
All my love—

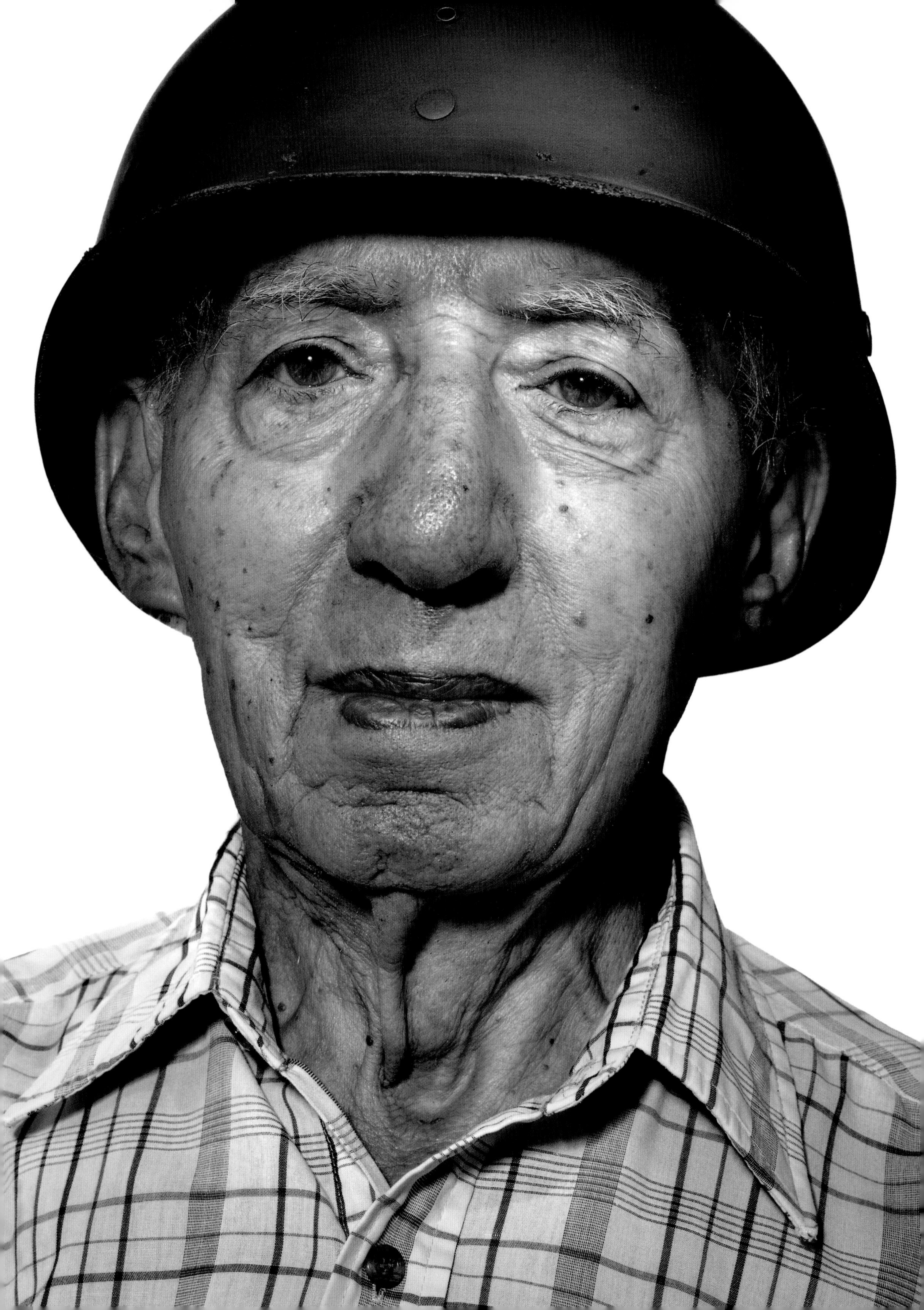

WHEN THE DRAFT CAME, I WAS working as an upholsterer in Queens. A friend of mine asked me to volunteer, and I said, "No, I'll wait until I'm drafted." About a month later I got my letter. Of course, he got to stay in the U.S. and I went overseas. I was the unit corporal in a cannon company attached to the infantry. When the invasion came we were the second group to go in and relieve the paratroopers in Normandy. If they needed fire in certain areas, we would give them the location and tell them where to fire. We walked into a nice little town when we first got there. Really pretty. I was eatin' some grapes from the vine when a tank came. We had to run. It chased us into a house. It must have been his house, because he wouldn't bomb us. We couldn't get out of there for five days.

When they transferred me to the infantry, I became a platoon sergeant. I had to teach some fellas all about the guns. I always liked to help people—I enjoyed it. And my platoon, I could have asked them to do anything and they would do it. No squawks or nothin', because I treated them right.

In another town, the lieutenant and I were in the basement of a two-family house. It was safe—solid concrete overhead. He says, "Dom, stay here tonight." And I said, "No. No, I don't want to stay here. I have to stay with my men." The platoons were on the first two floors. I went outside and when I was no more than two yards from the door, a bomb went through the house. It went through the place—didn't hurt anybody upstairs, but everybody in the basement was killed.

When we relieved the 28th Infantry in the Hürtgen Forest,[1] I was up on a hill and spotted a stream below. I could hear them hammering down there. I saw men walking around with baby carriages. And I realized afterward what it was. They were preparing for the Battle of the Bulge—carrying materials to build a place where tanks could pass over the water.[2]

That's where I got to be paralyzed. We were bombed, and I fell down the steps and hurt my arm.

Dominic Calabrese (left) stationed at Fort Bragg, NC.

I would pick it up with my other hand and it would just drop. My lieutenant says, "This is no good. You can't write, you can't do anything. Let's send you back to the medic, try to see what's wrong with your arm." They sent me home because I couldn't heal. When I got home, the war was over.

My greatest joy is to help people. This side of me developed in the Army, because a lot of them fellas that were drafted didn't understand what was goin' on. They were scared. I still like to take care of people, still do it today. If someone in my retirement community needs help, I help them. Like, you know, when we're eating and there are people in wheelchairs. To sit at the table, they have to move chairs, and even though I'm eatin', I get up. If you treat somebody the way you want to be treated, you'll have a lot of good people.

---

1 The Hürtgen Forest, near Aachen, Germany, was the setting of one of the most savage and drawn-out battles of World War II, the height of the conflict coming between September and December 1944. By its official end in February 1945, the battle had claimed twenty-four thousand American soldiers.

2 Hürtgen Forest served as a staging area for the German Ardennes Offensive, also known as the Battle of the Bulge. Taking place between December 1944 and January 1945, the Battle of the Bulge was the last major German offensive in World War II. Seeking to prevent the advance of the Allied line, Hitler ordered his commanders to launch an attack in the Ardennes region of Belgium, Luxembourg, and France. Despite initial success in driving the Allied line back (the "bulge"), a lack of resources prevented German forces from going further. It was the largest battle fought by American troops, with the casualties numbering over eighty thousand, and approximately nineteen thousand American soldiers killed.

"We were not really prepared for the Japanese when they bombed us early in the morning. It was still dark and we were asleep in our cots. We jumped into our foxholes and started shooting in a panic! I remember we hit a couple. The airplanes kept coming and strafing our troops until around dawn—we were told to withdraw and not defend our positions any longer. Then we heard the news that there was an order to surrender."

— **Ernie CORTEZ**

Peace with Honor

Ernie CORTEZ

First Lieutenant, U.S. Army

I WAS BORN AND RAISED IN THE PHILippines. When the war broke out, I was just out of high school, and my brothers and I worked in my father's bakery. In the mornings I went into the mountains to pick fruit from the trees so my mother could sell guavas and bananas from a little basket. That's how we maintained our livelihood. There wasn't much news about the war.

All I knew was that the Japanese started bombing Hawaii, and since we were an American outpost, they started to bomb Manila, too. We heard the Japanese would be returning from the north of the Philippines, so a strategy was devised to send defenses to Bataan—there was a peninsula there that served as a good access point. Ideally, when the Japanese came over, we could move to Australia from there. But it never happened that way.

I was freshly appointed to the position of recruiting officer when the Americans arrived. There was a great deal of preparation for merging my outfit with the National Guard from California. I was the commander of one hundred and twenty Philippine soldiers, and I assisted in the manning of the anti-aircraft guns. We worked with them to make the gun emplacements and dug foxholes wherever we stopped while moving backward from Bataan to Manila.

We were not really prepared for the Japanese when they bombed us early in the morning. It was still dark and we were asleep in our cots. We jumped into our foxholes and started shooting in a panic! I remember we hit a couple. The airplanes kept coming and strafing our troops until around dawn—we were told to withdraw and not defend our positions any longer. Then we heard the news that there was an order to surrender.

Our gun emplacements were high in the hills and mountains, and we had to pull them out. The Japanese told us to come down the hills to the road to start marching. It was a very hot day in April, and whenever we came across a river or stream, individual soldiers would stray away from the march to get a drink of water. The water was kind of oily, because there were a lot of dead soldiers up in the hill where the stream originated. That's why people got sick with malaria, dysentery, and all kinds of diseases. Soldiers who tried to get out of the column were knocked to the ground by Japanese rifles.[1]

At night we witnessed Japanese drivers heading to Bataan to mobilize near Corregidor Island. They drove recklessly, and numerous soldiers got run over. The drivers didn't care who they hit or what happened to the ones who got run over, because the people in the march were in bad condition—some were limping, some were wounded, and some were very sick on account of the water.

During the march I found two of my classmates from high school, and we started to plan an escape. We heard that there were fishermen along the beach who stopped in at nighttime to pick up any soldiers who wanted to get across Manila Bay to a civilian province unoccupied by the Japanese soldiers. We had to plan quickly, because we saw columns of smoke ahead of us. We thought, "Well, maybe the Americans are coming," because the radio always said that help was coming from America. We decided that by sundown we would cross an open field which was about four hundred feet to the shoreline.

When darkness came and the guards were marching fifteen feet apart, the three of us got out of the line and went toward the beach. There were ditches we would duck into while crossing the field. Thankfully the beaches were wooded and we found an abandoned hut containing civilian clothes. A fisherman came around, and showed us the mounds on the shore covered with crosses. He said, "See these mounds? This is where the escapees were shot, killed, and buried." I had money in my belt because I was given three months pay while I was in Bataan, so we contracted with this fisherman to take us across. When we were in the boat, it was very dark and we heard Japanese flying over Manila Bay. The fisherman told us that if they came too close, we'd capsize the boat, go under it, and breathe through the air pocket. But they never spotted us, so we were able to paddle our way across the bay to safety.

Pampanga province was crowded with civilians and soldiers. We were already in civilian clothing, but a man approached us soon after we arrived. He asked, "Do you know how they can recognize that you are soldiers?"

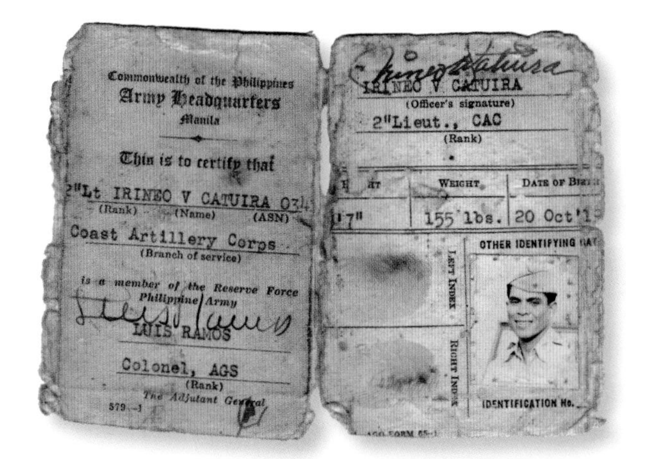

Commonwealth of the Philippines
Army Headquarters
Manila

This is to certify that
2"Lt IRINEO V CATUIRA
(Rank) (Name) (ASN)
Coast Artillery Corps
(Branch of service)
is a member of the Reserve Force
Philippine Army
LUIS RAMOS
Colonel, AGS
(Rank)
The Adjutant General
579-1

IRINEO V CATUIRA
(Officer's signature)
2"Lieut., CAC
(Rank)
WEIGHT
155 lbs.
LEFT INDEX
RIGHT INDEX
IDENTIFICATION No.

Ernie Cortez' original military ID; he changed his name from Irineo Caturia when he attended University of California Berkeley and found others had difficulty pronouncing his name.

Well, we didn't know. He said, "Look at your feet." Our feet were kind of white, while the rest of our bodies were dark. That's how the Japanese could pick out the escaped soldiers. We traveled along the outskirts, making our way from town to town by riding boats from one fishpond to another. While we were traveling, we met another gentleman in the fields, and he told us to go to his mother's place to eat rice and fish! They took good care of us there.

The gentleman knew about all the Japanese roadblocks and the way the soldiers searched *calessas*—horse-drawn, covered wagons that could carry six people—to capture escapees. He rode with us and guided us to the transportation company in Manila that would take us to our hometown province of Rizal. We took a different route instead of going through the areas where passengers were being screened. When I got to my hometown of Tanay, I saw that my father was very ill. He hardly recognized me when I arrived in the night.

I was around ninety pounds when I got home. I was trembling so much from malaria, they could put a hot rock on my body and I wouldn't feel it. My friends had to get a vine from the mountains, which was the natural substitute for the quinine pills. It had to be boiled until all the juice came out, and it tasted very bitter. It took a while to recover, and I was too sick to attend my father's funeral.

My mom was very scared, because she had three sons, all in hiding. When the Japanese army trucks passed through, they grabbed any men on the way to help them unload the ammunition and food going to the mountains. When we heard the trucks coming, my mom would say "Oh, speed up!" My brothers would run into their hiding spots. And here I was bedridden—didn't even have the strength to hide. During the occupation, everyone was under suspicion.

Our town had a growing underground freedom fighter group, and in order to find out who they were, everyone was put in a church and kept there for several nights. They let us out one by one. Before exiting, a guy with a paper bag on his head, with holes cut out for his eyes pointed, at certain people. They tied the people he chose to a horse and pulled them around town—parading them and their pain to set an example that there should be no resistance to the Japanese during their occupation.

I immigrated to the United States in 1948 and joined the U.S. Army Reserve. I was about to be shipped to Korea, but the war ended right as we arrived in southern California to be shipped off. I was still classified as a Korea veteran because I served three years in the reserve force of the U.S. Army. After that, I realized the value of a college degree and took an entrance examination, which admitted me into Berkeley.

I met my wife in the States. A friend who worked in the Oakland post office said, "Hey, I know a Filipino girl, she goes to my wife's laundry shop." It turned out she was a guerilla nurse in a neighboring province during World War II, but I met her at a Chinese laundry in Oakland.

---

1 On April 9th, 1942, American and Filipino soldiers charged with the defense of the islands of Luzon, Corregidor, and the Philippines were ordered to surrender to Japanese forces. Over seventy thousand troops in the province of Bataan were forcibly marched sixty miles over the course of a week to prisoner camps in the province of Tarlac. Undernourished and ill, vulnerable to extreme heat and thirst, and subjected to physical abuse, torture, and execution, thousands died along the way.

"Before I immigrated to the United States, I was a chef at the French Culinary Institute and then served in the French Navy. I enlisted because I was proud to be an American."

Michel CARTIER, Staff Sergeant, U.S. Army Air Corps

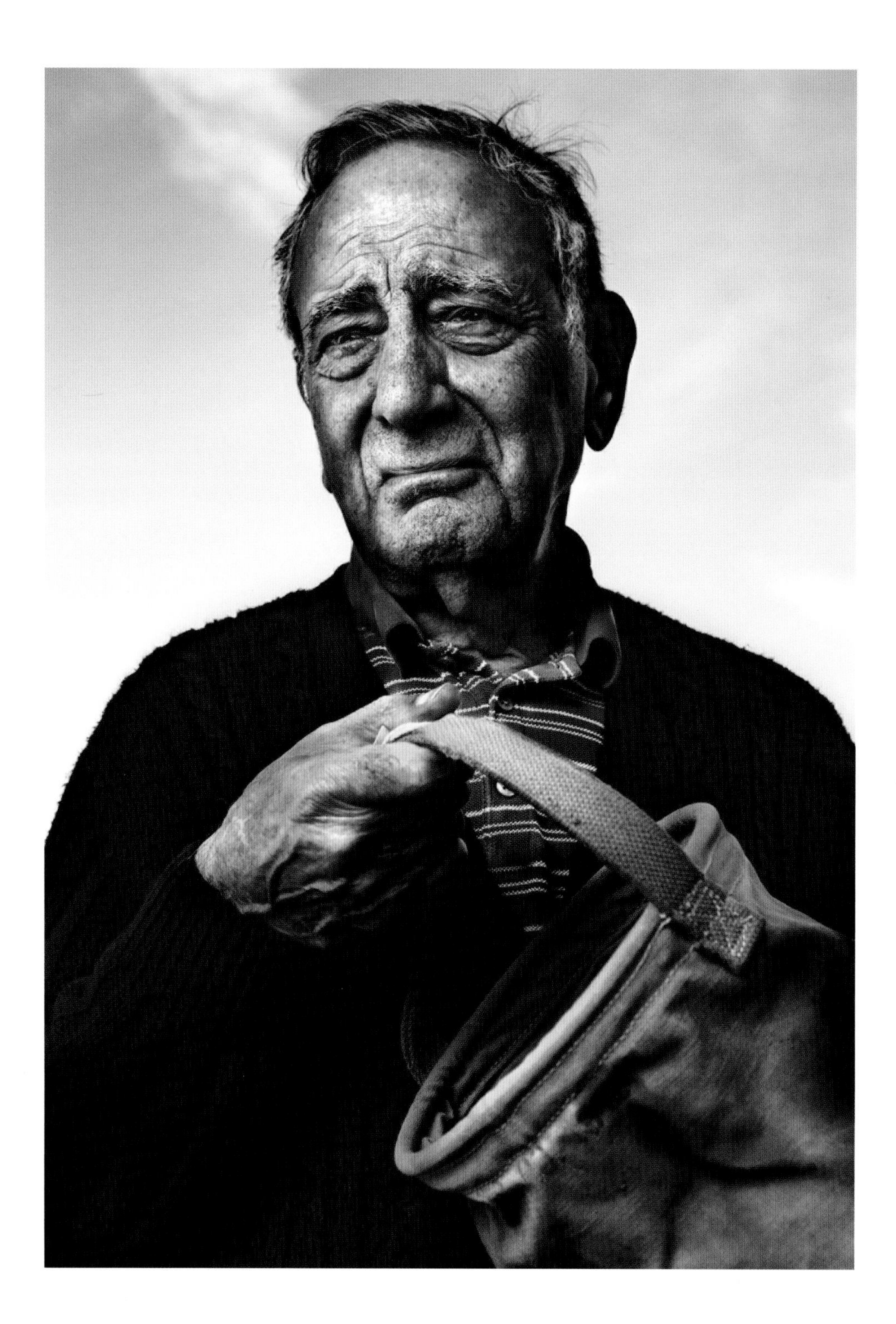

Above: **John LAMBROSE, Seaman, U.S. Navy** Opposite: **Francis "Smitty" SMITH, Staff Sergeant, U.S. Army Air Corps**

TOKYO ROSE USED TO CALL US "The Mystery Ship" because we could submerge twenty feet under water.[1] We listened to her radio show every night on the USS *Gunston Hall*, because she was the only female voice we had access to! She spoke beautiful English. She was born in Los Angeles and had gone to college in California. She was telling us—with great pleasure—how we were going to lose the war. She knew right where we were, almost all the time. But of course we knew we were going to win the war all along. What the Japanese didn't realize was that their propaganda—the radio shows and the funny illustrations they drew of us and littered over our ships—was incredibly entertaining. Those things gave us energy!

We made five invasions with the Marine Corps and four with the Army. I was a gunner through all of them, and I don't think I ever really got scared. Hell, at nineteen—you're excited, man! You think you can live forever! 'Course, when you get a little age on you, when you're twenty-five or thirty, that changes. We had boys on our ship that were thirty years old—we called them "Pops!"

We didn't really get into action until the invasion of Leyte in the Philippines.[2] That's where I saw my first kamikaze. After about one hundred and fifty days—invading the Marshall Islands, New Guinea, Weetaw, Palau, Guam, Iwo Jima, Okinawa—we'd been through more than one hundred kamikaze raids. Kamikaze showers! The Japanese—they already had their burial rites and everything. If they went back home, it was a no-no. Oh, no, no, they would never go back. Besides, they didn't have enough gas.

We put one hundred thousand miles on my ship during the war and didn't even get off at a single port. It was crazy, but we learned to live with it. Young people can adjust to pretty much anything. Every now and then we'd get in a scuffle, and we'd just wipe our noses, and move on. I tell you what I missed—something good to eat. When I got back into Honolulu, first thing I got was waffles and syrup. Waffles are the thing I missed most during the war.

After the war, I was interested in college and finding a career that best suited me. I wouldn't have been as interested if it hadn't been for the war—it changed my life. I started working for the Boy Scouts of America in 1952 and really got to liking it. I ended up becoming their third Scout Executive since 1910. I had forty people working under me and three thousand volunteers doing a heck of a lot of work for free. I scheduled motivational speakers to come talk to the Scouts, and one time a Marine lieutenant came and referred to me as his friend. Some young mothers in the crowd started speaking out against war; one said, "Someday your daughters will marry Scouts!" I totally understood their reaction—war isn't something you like to associate a young kid with. But I don't believe the Boy Scouts have anything to do with soldier life. All we wanted those boys to learn was how to build character. Now, I also think that the more character and honor you have, the better suited you are to become a soldier.

Machinist's Mate Second Class, U.S. Navy

---

1 Tokyo Rose was the name attributed to several female Japanese radio broadcasters who operated during wartime with the intent of negatively impacting the morale of American soldiers. The person most closely identified with the name is Iva Toguri, a Japanese American citizen born in Los Angeles who had been visiting a relative in Japan when war was declared. Stranded, she was pressured by the Japanese government to renounce her U.S. citizenship. After refusing, Toguri went to work for Radio Tokyo, eventually hosting a program called *The Zero Hour*, which was produced by Allied prisoners of war.

After the surrender of Japan, journalists offered money to interview the infamous Tokyo Rose. In need of money, Toguri came forward. She was subsequently arrested and tried on eight counts of treason. Convicted of one count, she served eight years of a ten-year sentence. Ultimately, it was revealed that two of her colleagues at Radio Tokyo who had testified against her had been pressured into lying on the stand, and Toguri was pardoned by President Gerald Ford in 1976.

2 The island of Leyte, in the Philippines, was the location for two significant battles in World War II. The Battle of Leyte, in October 1944, was the starting point of the Philippines campaign, the goal of which was to free the Philippines of Japanese occupiers and pave the way to the island of Luzon, and ultimately Japan. Simultaneously, the Battle of the Leyte Gulf occurred offshore. The largest naval battle of World War II, it resulted in the Imperial Japanese Navy sustaining massive losses to their fleet.

"We have a counterintelligence community here in southern California. Every guy has got a story to tell. We still get together every two months in Anaheim and swap stories about our experiences."

— Don ALECOCK

I WASN'T EVEN BIG ENOUGH TO BE A soldier. I was only ninety-seven pounds, and you had to weigh 113 to be a soldier. The old-fashioned non-commissioned officers came up to San Pedro from Panama to train us. They took me under their wing and helped me along until I finished my training. From there, they sent me to radar school on a little island off the coast of North Carolina. I was going to a highly technical school, very top secret—you couldn't even write the word "radar." If you did, out you went. When I arrived, they promoted me to section chief and I headed a crew of twenty people.

We joined forces with General Patton's group to do training in the Mojave Desert, and it was hell, it would get up to one hundred degrees at midnight. From there we went up to a mountainous area near Palm Springs, and they gave us a radar unit as big as a whole room, which we used to track the aircraft flying out of March Air Force Base, picking them up as they took off and following their course.[1] One night we were tracking a plane that we thought was acting unusual and decided to turn the searchlight on to get a read on it. The light was a powerful thing. You could read a magazine from ten miles away with it. Unbeknownst to us, the plane was piloted by the general in command of March, and when we put the light on him, it reflected in multiple directions within the cockpit—completely blinding him during his flight. Finally he got the word through to our radio section to shut the damn thing off. I thought that was the end of my rising military career, but the Army is full of surprises.

Alecock prior to leaving New York Harbor for convoy duty.

I joined a signal unit heading overseas on an old tobacco boat. After a terrible fourteen-day journey across the Atlantic, while all the German subs were busting the hell out of things, we eventually ended up at our post in England. It was a racetrack with horse stables for barracks. We kept our weapons, canteens, helmets, and what they call "web equipment" in the troughs. We joined up with the Army units and started getting ready for the invasion.

On one of the first days, the captain came up to me with a job: "Go draw a weapon, a jeep, and a driver and come back here." When I returned to his office, he patted a footlocker and he asked, "You know what that is?" I nodded, and he said, "Well, look inside." The footlocker was filled with crystals worth hundreds of thousands of dollars. He told me to take the locker down to Portsmouth Harbour.[2] When I arrived, there were thousands of Americans! Everyone was preparing for D-Day. They had tanks lined up for miles, and alongside them, equipment, gasoline trucks, and wreckers to pull them out. You couldn't get between them, it was so tightly packed. Every few miles, the MPs would stop us and read our orders—and I was very high-priority that day. We turned our footlocker over to their communications people, and they took out all the old crystals from the radios and put these new crystals in. They filtered what you said at a particular frequency, and stopped the Germans from listening to our troops. You put one crystal in for transmitting and another one for receiving. The German Army Intelligence had big trucks along the water in France listening to us—but that day they were denied access.

After the heavy losses following D-Day, there was a shortage of officers. They needed new ones, so I went in for an interview and they selected me. It was a big jump to go from sergeant to officer. I was what they called a

Don Alecock (middle) sharing field rations with fellow soldiers during a training mission.

"mustang"—which is a nickname for officers who didn't have to go to officer school. They sent me back down to Cherbourg, France, during the invasion and put me in an outfit with five hundred German POWs. Our job was to sift through everything building up on the beach to see if it could be used in the war: wire, crystals, medical equipment. We had the Germans scour through it all. Copper wire, for instance, was almost as valuable as gold. They hadn't had any copper wire for about three years in France. People were stealing it and selling it on the black market. They had me go out and see what was going on, and I'd see GIs with giant rolls of bills.

Later on, they transferred me to Army Intelligence and I became a special agent. In Europe, Army Intelligence corresponded with the FBI on everything. In contrast, in the Pacific, MacArthur didn't want to use them. He wanted his own men, not people someone sent in. We did all of the investigation on soldiers, civilians, politicians, and even on the women who were marrying the GIs. They were investigated to make sure that they weren't from some kind of an organization that wanted to overthrow the U.S. So here I was, not even big enough to be a soldier, and I wound up a retired captain!

We have a counterintelligence community here in southern California. Every guy has got a story to tell. We still get together every two months in Anaheim and swap stories about our experiences.

---

1 Built during the anticipation of entry into World War I, March Air Force Base supported up to seventy-five thousand troops at the height of World War II, and was the final training site of many bombardment groups before reporting to duty in the Pacific.

2 Portsmouth Harbour was a military embarkation point for the D-Day landings on June 6, 1944. Southwick House, just to the north of Portsmouth, had been chosen as the headquarters for the Supreme Allied Commander, U.S. General Dwight D. Eisenhower, during D-Day.

Captain, U.S. Army

THE NEW YORK TIMES BESTSELLER
D-DAY
JUNE 6,
1944:
THE CLIMACTIC BATTLE OF
WORLD WAR II

IF YOU'RE GOING TO BE A BALL TURret gunner, you can't be a small guy. I wasn't too tall, but I was big enough to become a gunner in a B-17 Flying Fortress.[1] My first mission out of England was on D-Day in 1944. I ended up flying twenty-six missions with a crew of ten other guys. We bombed in France, Poland, Romania, Italy—we had no problems until September 5th, over Stuttgart, Germany. The flak hit us, two engines went out, and we were losing altitude—there was no way we'd get back to England. When we realized we were close to the Swiss border, we crash-landed in a small airport there. The Swiss came out and cheerfully greeted us as I dropped out of my turret—which had fallen through a house on the way down.

My crew and I were sent up into Adelboden, which was an internment camp up in the Alps.[2] We all lived in very fancy hotels because it was a tourist town. It wasn't too bad, but we still wanted to go home. After about six months, a tail gunner from my crew ran into some Yugoslavs. At that time in Switzerland, Yugoslavs were allowed to run free, and they were all over the place. They were trying to make some money, so they offered to get us out of Switzerland and into France. Well, me and another guy sat on that for a few days and said, "Yeah, let's do that!"

It was spring, and in the middle of the night they quickly took us down the mountain to a train station. Of course, we were in civilian clothes and got on the train without any problem. They took us up to Bern, Switzerland. From there we were alone, but we traveled by train to another town where people were waiting to meet us.

Once there, they found us and hid us up in an attic. The next day, they woke us up and pointed toward bicycles on the street. They guided us as we rode the bikes for three or four miles. There were all kinds of people coming in one direction or another, looking for work, and we were riding along with them.

Finally, we came to a farmhouse, and they told us to get up in the barn and stay there. They said, "We will let you know when it is time—we will tell you, *go, go, go*." When that day came, we ran across the field, jumped over a barbed-wire fence, and we wound up in France. We headed south to Nice to avoid the Nazis, and from there we caught a British cargo plane back to our base in Framingham, England.

After that whole adventure, I was interrogated because I was an escapee out of Switzerland and France. The British pumped us a bit to see that we were really who we said we were—were we Americans, did we know our baseball, stuff like that. It was a strange story, and they wanted to make sure that they understood it properly and that it was all true. Once they got the facts down, they sent me home to Massachusetts.

Military portrait of James Eckman.

ORDER of the LUCKY BASTARDS

This is to certify that

S/Sgt. James B. Eckman

the above airman; having been disabled over enemy territory, and having landed on the "neutral soil of Switzerland," has fullfilled the necessary requirements, and is hereby accepted into this most sacred and propitious order. — the lucky bastard —

1. Nantes, Fr.	9. Merseburg, Gr.	17. Stuttgart, Gr.
2. Misburg, Gr.	10. Pas de Calais, Fr	18. Merseburg, Gr.
3. Spieka, Gr.	11. Munich, Gr.	19. Neuvy-sur-Loire, Fr.
4. Fallersleben, Gr.	12. Munich, Gr.	20. Rahmel, Gr.
5. Berlin, Gr.	13. Munich, Gr.	21. Trzebinia, Poland
6. Paris, Fr.	14. Area 9, Fr.	22. Zilistea, Rumania
7. Bohlen, Gr.	15. Schweinfurt, Gr.	23. Toulouse, Fr.
8. Gien, Fr.	16. Merseburg, Gr.	24. Brest, Fr.
25. Isle of Sylt, Gr.	26. Stuttgart, Gr.	

Membership card for The Order of the Lucky Bastards, a club formed by Eckman's navigator after their internment in Switzerland.

Staff Sergeant, U.S. Army Air Corps

1 A four-engine heavy bomber, the B-17 Flying Fortress was used in strategic bombing campaigns, primarily against German industrial and military targets.

2 During this time, American prisoners of war in Switzerland were typically held in three places: Adelboden, Wengen, and Davos. Enlisted men were held at Adelboden and Wengen, while officers went to Davos. Many Swiss internment camps were converted ski resorts or tourist towns.

"You can't understand the full context of a comrade until you completely realize that the man standing next to you is willing to offer his life to protect you."

Opposite: **Irv ROLLER, Corporal, U.S. Army**
Following spread: **Barney SCHUSSEL, Staff Sergeant, U.S. Army; John REID, Sergeant, U.S. Army**

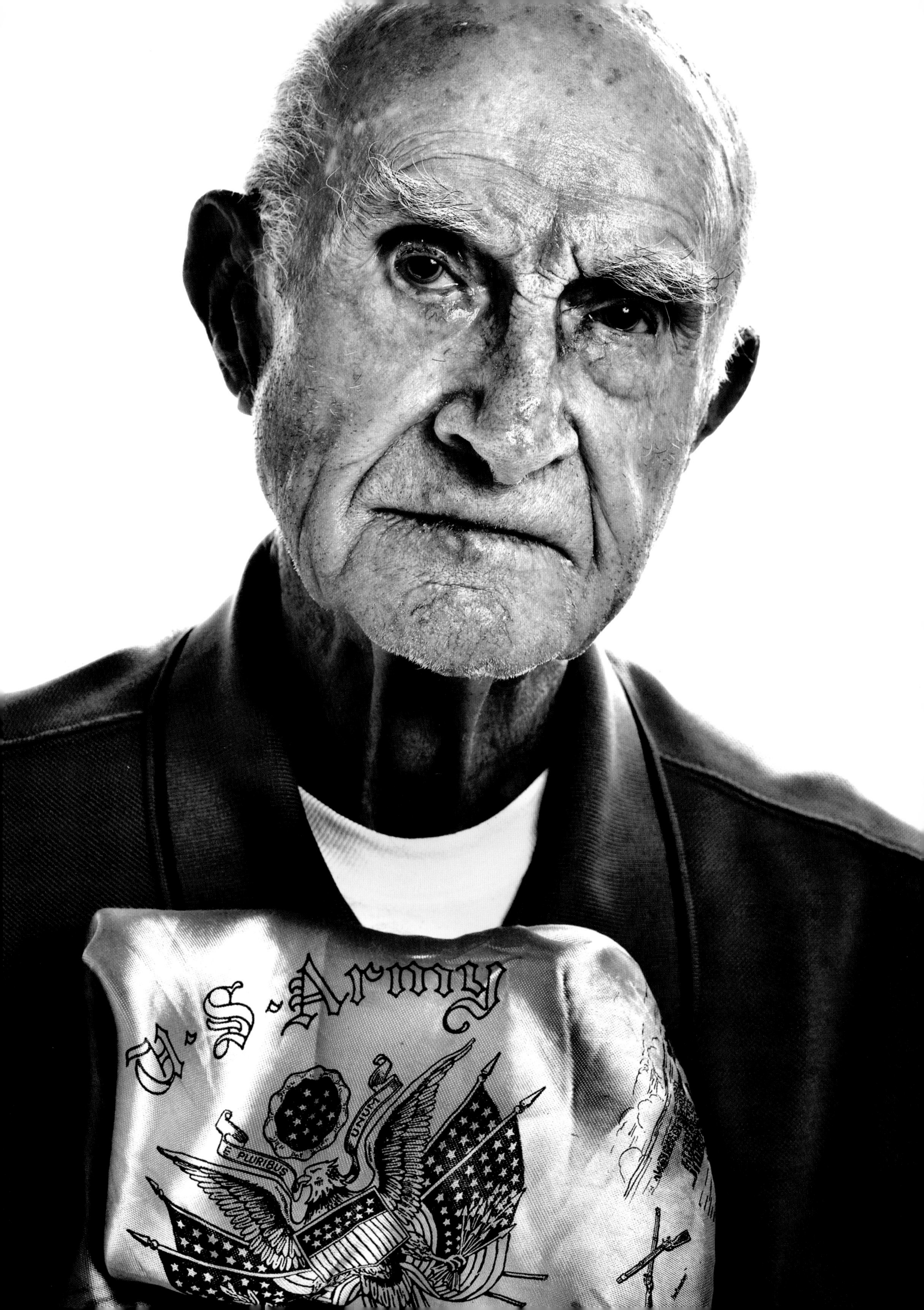
U·S·Army
E PLURIBUS UNUM

Panora Ltd., London, W.C.1.

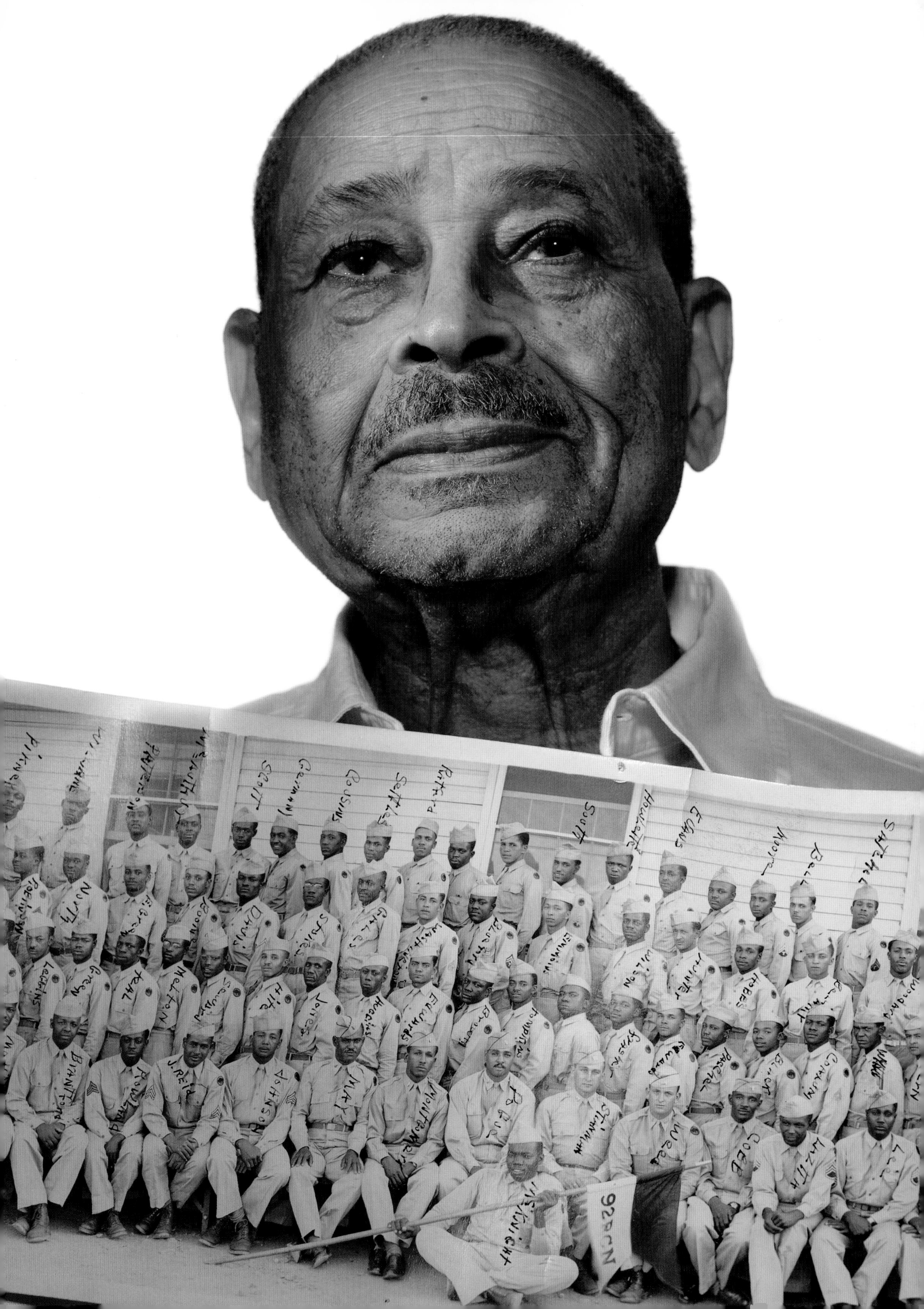
Scott
Cousins
Settles
North
Davis
Green
Jones
Edwards
Wilson
Hunter
Bell
J. Reid
Johnson
Montgomery

Robert WATSON

A WEEK BEFORE THE INVASION OF Normandy, we were in Liverpool, England, doing training in landing craft, going through our routine as beachmasters.[1] All the responsibilities on the beach—medical, communications, engineering, demolition, traffic control—fell to our crew. On June the second we were gathered together in a huge valley. There were about four thousand of us. There was a general on top of a tank up on the hillside there, and he proceeded to tell us, "We are now going to invade the continent of Europe." He told us we were the best-equipped and the best-trained army in the world and we were going to "win one for the USA." He told us that airborne troops would land at 0200 hours behind enemy lines, and at 0300, the Navy guns would open up with huge cannon fire. He said that the Air Force would come over and bomb the shore batteries, and they would send one hundred tanks for immediate firepower. He told us they had platform rocket ships they would send in that would pulverize the shore batteries.

The Air Force missed Omaha Beach entirely; the Navy guns went up over the top and past the watchtowers, into the fields and pastures behind them.[2] The rockets went helter-skelter and never touched that beach. Those tanks all sank. We've got boats loaded with eighteen-, nineteen-, twenty-year-olds who have never been in battle before, never saw anybody die before, had no idea in the world what was going to happen. The landing craft I was in hit a mine, and it tore the front end completely off and apart. Fifty men were killed immediately, that's a reasonable estimate. What was left of the landing craft went up in the air; it tore up my leg and I went flying into the water. The underwater demolition people had boats in the area, and I got in one of those. While all this was happening, many, many more boats were going into the beach, and some of them were making it and landing on the beach itself, but those didn't get very far. The German defensive positions were one hundred percent operational. If my landing craft had made it to the beach successfully, there would have been a pile of bodies. It was just a terrible, terrible situation. But I did get to the water's edge and through that mess: the stink, the smell, the smoke, the noise, bodies and body parts, arms, legs, you name it. What bothered me most going up the beach—and I'll never forget it as long as I live—was all those voices: help me, somebody help me, over here, medic, medic, somebody help me!

I took charge of a bulldozer and a crew of half a dozen. We would move down the beach with the tide and clear an area two hundred feet wide, creating a driveway so that the landing craft would have a safe way to get to the beach. As the tide receded, the landing craft that made it to the beach would get stuck in the sand after they unloaded. So the coxswain of that landing craft would send his gunner over: "Get that bulldozer and get me the hell out of here!" And I would tell his gunner, "You go back and tell your coxswain he's going to stay right here with me. When you get it loaded one hundred percent with wounded, that's when I'll push you back in." Me and two other bulldozers, we took kids off that beach that morning, out there to the hospital ships. It was just an amazing thing to get those kids out of there.

We stayed on the beach for twenty-eight days. We'd lost fifty, sixty men; there were another fifty of us that kept getting beat and battered but were able to stay on station. We were real short-handed; we couldn't have spared anybody. I decided that if this was where I was going to be, I was going to be the best damn sailor in this outfit. I got the job done. I was promoted three times in ten and a half months, while I was still eighteen. There was no question in my mind that I was going to be in the service, and there was no question in my mind that wherever I was and wherever I landed, I was going to do what I had to do.

---

1 The invasion of western Europe by Allied forces was codenamed Operation Overlord. The first stage of the invasion was a massive amphibious landing on the coast of Normandy, France, on June 6, 1944. Known as D-Day, the invasion involved five thousand ships and over one hundred and seventy thousand troops landing on a fifty-mile stretch of coast.

2 Omaha Beach was the codename for a section of the Normandy coast used as a landing point in the D-Day invasion. The assault by Allied forces had to contend with heavy seas, obstacles and mines in the water and on land, and well-prepared German defenses, including artillery and machine guns, along the coast and cliffs above. Poor weather contributed to Allied bombers missing their coastal targets, the pre-landing bombardment from the Navy was not extensive enough, and the rough seas prevented many amphibious tanks from reaching the shore.

Seaman First Class, U.S. Navy

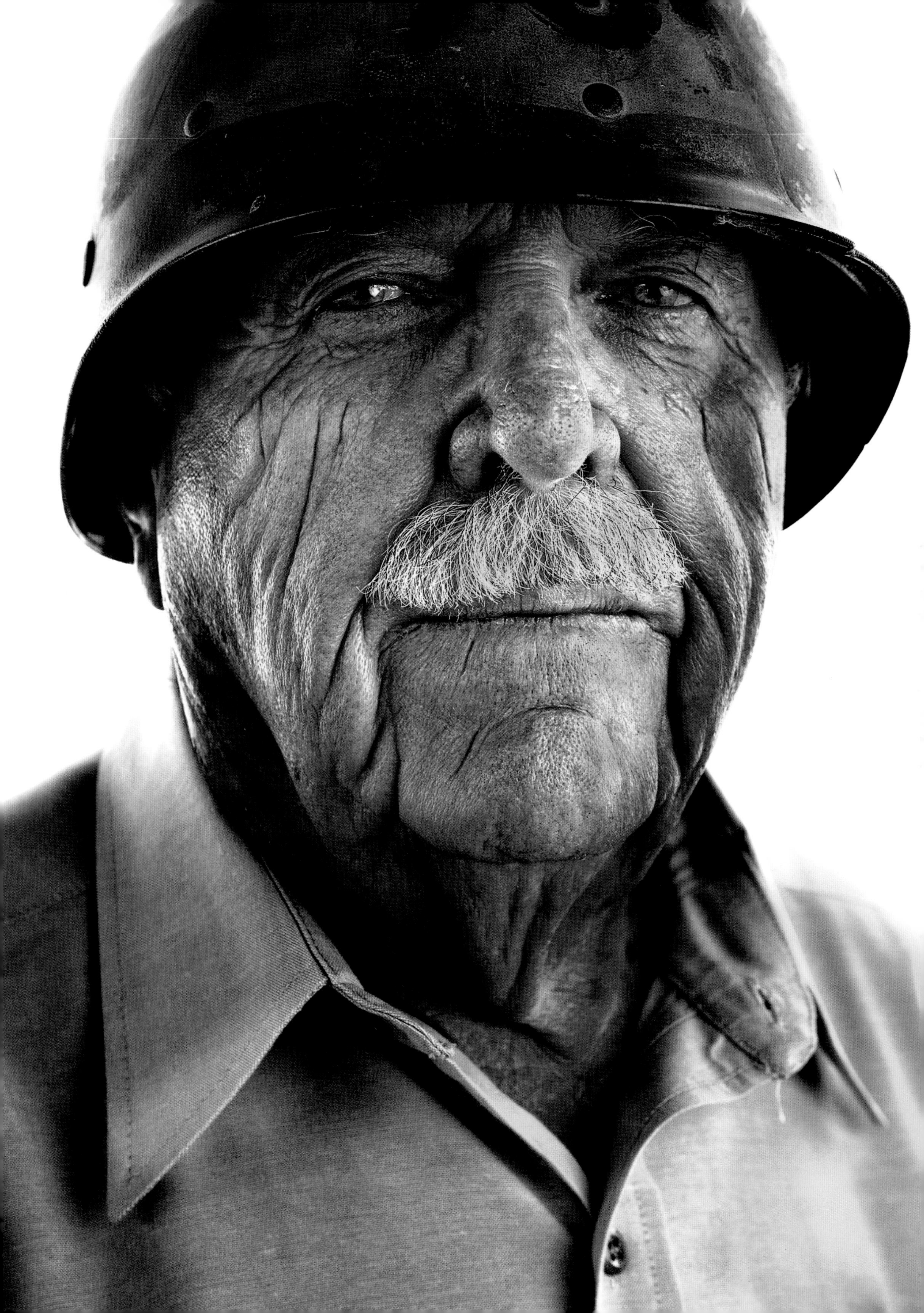

Military portrait of Dominic Zappia, 1940.

Dominic ZAPPIA

ANYBODY THAT SAYS THEY WEREN'T scared, they're liars. It was during the nighttime there in Normandy when no American planes were allowed to fly. We did two-hour shifts on the gun mount, then we'd go back to sleep, and then back on a gun mount. If they dropped a bomb, it would go *eeeeeeeeeerrrrrrrr*. Your whole body just tightened up. You tightened up like a zip, like a vice.

There are only four men left from my ship who were in the Normandy invasion.[1] See, I go to reunions. Normandy, Iwo Jima. I go to several every year, and they aren't cheap! But it's worth it because I get to see the guys. And that's where we meet, the original ship. She's sixty-five years out of commission now—a mothball. They just keep her tied up to pier and take care of her. Five days of memorial services, banquets, dancing, a bell ceremony for all those who passed away. Most guys can't fit into their old uniforms, so they just wear sports coats and slacks—but I was able to get into mine, medals and everything.

I've been in the Navy my whole life. I was ranked Chief Boatswain's Mate. That's right next to the captain. I participated in the Korean and Vietnam wars. I was aboard the ship that took part in the Cuban crisis. The Bay of Pigs. In 1962 I went to Johnson Island to do the nuclear testing of a missile—and they called it the "Dominic Operation" after me.

I lost friends in the service, but I don't talk about that. That's why it's taking me this long to start writing a book. I started over a month ago. I've been working a little bit every day. I just got done with Valley Forge 1965. I'm trying to remember everything, you know. Like, I hate to talk about it, but on the USS *Hancock*, we had the son of the golden arches—McDonald's. He was on our ship. Well, one morning they're on the ship calculating everything with the stars, and they elevate the gun to the position to check it out. He was underneath the gun mount up in the bridge. They elevated the gun and it came down on him, twisted his spinal cord. This was in Hong Kong. They had to take him to the hospital, and we don't know what ever happened to him. Things like that happen, you know. He was a good friend of mine.

A lot people are against the wars happening now, but I'm not. My attitude is: if we don't take care of that end over there, they're gonna come over here and take care of us. In fact, I believe that—just like in Israel and other countries—kids should have to do two years of service. That'll either make 'em or break 'em.

---

1 See pg. 64, footnote 1.

Chief Boatswain's Mate, U.S. Navy

Above: **Earl FOUTS, Sergeant, U.S. Army** Opposite: **Larry LINDLOW, First Lieutenant, U.S. Air Force**
Following spread: **David BROWN, Technician Third Grade, U.S. Army; Bill RISKO, Corporal, U.S. Marines**

Irving PHILLIPS

INITIALLY I WAS AGAINST THE WAR because I was influenced by my philosophy as a socialist. I believed in a class struggle, that wars were fought for profits and markets, and that the only ones to gain from the wars were the capitalists who owned the factories. In retrospect, this was a very simplistic view of Marxist thinking. I was also a pacifist and believed in it sincerely. Eventually I became aware of Hitler and what he was doing to the Jews, and that certainly added another dimension to my thinking. When the draft came, I couldn't honestly say I was a conscientious objector, and I entered the Army.

I learned my Marxism in Boston Common. In 1929, when I was fourteen, I was selling newspapers on Tremont Street. I was yelling, "Read about the Great Depression!" or "Read about the great stock market crash!" I didn't know what I was saying. Soapboxes used to assemble every Sunday. Marxist Labor Party, Communist Party, and the religious Salvationists—all preaching from their soapboxes on the mall. I tried it a few times, but I was more of listener than anything else. Alfred Baker Lewis, who was a leader of the Massachusetts Socialist Party, took a shining to me. He was also a millionaire. People would say, "You're a socialist. Why don't you give up your money?" And he would say, "When we have socialism, I'll give up my money." He had an answer, at least.

Military portrait of Phillips.

When I got drafted, they put me in charge of information and education. Of all things! "Here's a guy who's against the war, let's put him in charge of information and education." When I became the instructor, the war with Germany was pretty much over, and our efforts were being focused on Japan. I had to prepare the American troops for this invasion. It put me in a pretty tough spot. How was I going to explain this to these American soldiers who were committing their lives to invading Japan? Well, I tried to be objective about it. I didn't say the Japanese were terrible; I just focused on the reality. I didn't posture—I just pointed out that we had better troops, were better armed, had many more airplanes, had more tanks, and that therefore we would win.

I didn't try to label them as monsters or anything like that, which would have been the simplest thing. These guys knew they were going to fight. They liked my approach because I gave them a straight story. I didn't say anything really polarizing. I got the statistics on how strong we were, and how many aircrafts we had, and how many aircrafts the Japanese had. That was the best kind of reassurance.

I turned against the Marxist philosophy and became a socialist because the Marxists had become fanatical. I turned on Joe Stalin because he was a dictator.[1] So I never recognized Russia as a real socialist state; I recognized it as a communist state, a dictatorship. I was able to make that differentiation. One reason why the socialist movement never took root in this country was because of Franklin D. Roosevelt. He stole the platform of the Socialist party. He created social reform with what came to be known as the New Deal.[2]

Of course, I'm glad to be an American. And I only got to go to Harvard because of the G.I. Bill, which was thrilling for me. I majored in labor economics. The important thing for a nation is not so much a question of whether it's a socialist or communist state, but that it's a democracy. The fact that we have a two-party system here is a reflection of that. That's the important thing.

Technician Fourth Grade, U.S. Army

---

1 Joseph Stalin rose to power in Soviet Russia following the death of Vladimir Lenin. In the 1930s he consolidated his position as head of the Communist Party through the persecution and repression of elements deemed dangerous to the party, typically dissenters and political threats to the new regime, but also including artists, writers, and various social groups.

2 Responding to the economic crisis of the Great Depression, the New Deal was a series of reform programs implemented by President Roosevelt and Congress in the 1930s. Intended to mitigate the damage and put Americans back to work, the federal government oversaw many new domestic programs, including Public Works Administration, Social Security Act, and Works Progress Administrations, which provided almost eight million jobs between 1935 and 1943.

Above: **James STEVENS, Specialist First Class, U.S. Navy** Opposite: **Vernon ROBINSON, Sergeant, U.S. Army Air Corps**

TUSKEGEE AIRMEN
1949

Harold MASON

THE 146TH ENGINEERING COMPANY was the only topographic engineering company in the European Theater. Most engineering companies were assigned to combat or construction. We weren't attached to a division or regiment. We were always just in the Third Army.

I went to a high school in Chattanooga that specialized in mapping and civil engineering, and eventually I applied to the Corps of Engineers.[1] I was a topographic photogrammeter, which is somebody who uses area photographs to make elevation maps. I was fortunate when I got drafted in early '42, because that's exactly what I was assigned to do for them.

First they sent me all by my lonesome—I was a twenty-one-year-old kid—to Camp Claiborne in Alexandria, Louisiana. When I arrived, Camp Claiborne consisted of a telephone booth and a private first class. There was no Camp Claiborne. The PFC barked, "Turn around, go back to Alexandria, and stay at the hotel until somebody comes to get you." And that's just what I did. There were a number of guys there. We stayed there a couple of weeks until they came for us. When I arrived, the new engineering group had just been formed. I was the first one in besides the major, who was the battalion commander. There wasn't much happening. I befriended the engineering guys in the company next door, and they said, "Why don't you transfer over here, we got an opening." I made the transfer request and got it, only to find out we were going overseas immediately. My wife was on her way to Louisiana, but I was gone by the time she arrived, and I didn't see her again for nearly three years.

Being a topographic engineering company, we weren't in the front lines during the fighting. We went in on the first week of the invasions. We would fly over everything and photograph with oblique cameras—they shot sideways as well as straight down to offer three views, which gives you depth. Then you put all the maps together and converted them into an elevation map. These maps depicted the contours in terrain depth, bodies of water, density of forests, and roads. That's why it was so useful during the war.

We started in North Africa and pushed our way along the Mediterranean coast to access Sicily. I flew all over southern Italy in the B-24, taking photographs.[2] It's really a different world. Everything is made out of stone or earth, not much wood. They lived a much more humble life than we did here. For example, the farmers would bring all of their livestock into the house at night. Apparently when the Germans were occupying that part of Italy, they either killed or stole all their stock. I learned this when a farmer and his wife invited me to have dinner with them. I was shocked! Chickens, ducks, geese, and two sheep—all in the house.

I didn't make the Normandy invasion. I was sent home on a thirty-day leave in May 1945. I was sitting on the veranda of the Peabody Hotel in Memphis, eating a big dinner with my wife and friend. I had a little broadcast radio that I always carried around with me. The radio announced that the Normandy Invasion had begun and that weather was bad. I said, "Oh no! If it's all overcast, raining over there, and they don't have any air support—they're gonna get it up on those cliffs!" I knew the Germans had the Eighth Army all lined up there on the cliffs. It was hard to be away from it all, and I often wondered: why was I the first guy out of my company to be sent back?

It was a year later when I learned the answer. I ran into my former lieutenant in Hot Springs, Arkansas, right on the street. He was stationed in the Army-Navy hospital there. The first question I asked was: "Okay, Griff. How come I got to go home?" He said, "We put 146 names into a hat and drew. Yours was the first name!"

---

1 The United States Army Corps of Engineers is a federal agency that includes civilian and military personnel, and provides public engineering, design, and construction services in peace and wartime.

2 The B-24 Liberator was an American heavy bomber developed in 1939. The B-24 had a long range and high top speed, and had great success in operations in the Pacific, European, and African Theaters. More than eighteen thousand were produced, the largest quantity of aircraft built during the Second World War.

Sergeant, U.S. Army

Part I—Tues., Aug. 3, 1943
Los Angeles Examiner
ermany Fights to Avert Disaster on Two Fronts
Hitler's Todt battalions have built a defense wall around so-called "Fortress Europe." The Fuehrer has ordered that ery soldier be given shell proof cover. The west wall reaches m Kirkenes to Biarritz in France, is reported to be 75 miles p in places and consists of forts, pillboxes, bunkers, moats, on-teeth tank traps, many mine fields and barbed-wire en- ements.
The coast of Belgium is said to be one long blockhouse underground tunnels connecting three and four parallel walls fortifications in depth. The south and east wall, hastily built ce the United Nations occupied Africa, begins at the Spanish order, stretches along the coast of France, and crosses the delta the Rhone River Valley to the Alps. From there it traverses the River in Italy, guarding the many passes through the mountains. e fortress wall then runs along northern Yugoslavia and thence uth in the Morava-Vardar Valley to Macedonia. It protects the oast of Macedonia to Thrace, where the line changes, running orth through Bulgaria to the Carpathian Mountains in Rumania nd then through east Poland, Lithuania and Latvia to the Baltic.
Elaborate fortifications are not considered sufficient to ithstand a very determined attack. Realizing this, Hitler has reated a "Fortress Mobile," interior lines of communications to ove mechanized armies to any danger point.
FACED with disaster on two fronts, one of which is collapsing, Hitler's legions soon may suffer the Reich's second great setback of World War II.
The ousting of Mussolini, which caught Hitler and his strategists by surprise, presaged early surrender of Italy. But the Nazis apparently plan to make a stand along the Po River valley in northern Italy. To this end troops have poured through the Brenner Pass and the Italian towns of Trieste and Fiume, on the edge of Yugoslavia, have been occupied by German soldiers. This, say competent observers, indicates Hitler wants to protect the Brenner Pass, gateway to Germany, and the eastern shores of the Adriatic.
Meanwhile, Russian forces are smashing what is believed to have been a Nazi summer offensive, a drive aimed at Moscow, and hoped to be a swift ending to the war against the Soviet. Orel, key city in Germany's 1800-mile Russian front, is under violent attack and German troops there have been ordered to stop Soviet troops and 'prevent the complete defeat of the German army.
Thus in Italy and Russia the Germans are hard pressed.
Occupation of Italy by the Allies leaves the Balkans open to invasion, and the now shaky Balkans will be of little help to retreating Hitler.
Added to Hitler's worries is the bility that Turkey may join the Allies
Timed with a drive at Yugoslavia co be an attack on Nazi positions in Gree an attack starting from Egypt and sw ing Crete in its path. Participation o key in the war could bring a third p attack from across the Dardanelles.
A gigantic United Nations offensive is under way, threatening Hitler from the East and from the South. Germany itself is under heavy air attack. Her undersea war is diminishing.
Collapse of either the Russian or southern Europe front may be the beginning of the end for Hitler.
Arctic Ocean
SUPPLY LINE FROM AMERICA
Barents Sea
White Sea
NORWAY
SWEDEN
FINLAND
ESTONIA
LATVIA
Baltic Sea
North Sea
MOSCOW
Volga
Line of farthest German advance
SOVIET
RUSSIA
STALINGRAD
GERMANY
POLAND
HUNGARY
AUSTRIA
CAUCASUS
Caspian
SUPPLY ROUTE FROM UNITED STATES

"I learned more than I could have in fifteen universities. When I went in, I had absolutely no awareness of the world, politics and different cultures. I am grateful to have survived."

Edwin SAWICKI, Sergeant, U.S. Army

Will Roberts (front row, 4th from left) and the officers and enlisted men of the 1402nd Engineer Combat Battalion, Company B, 1953.

THE ARMY SENT US TO ITALY TO supply ammunition to troops on the front lines. We landed in Naples, where we lived in two-person pup tents for the first nine months. After that, we were scheduled to be a part of the invasion of Anzio, but about a week before it happened, they pulled us out because we were a black company.[1] The infantry didn't want blacks in there as their backup, even though we were the best ammo company over there in Italy.

As far as I know, there were three ammunition companies in Italy, but ours handled more than twice the ammunition that the other companies did. I believe we were the only company converting 155mm artillery shells into smoke shells. Smoke was an important tool. The artillery used the shells for cover and to smoke Germans out of hiding without completely demolishing the buildings. To convert the shells, we would remove the fuze and the booster from the projectile, then drill out the length of about a ten-inch blade, pack it with smoke, and re-boost them. We started out only making fifty a day and, by the fourth month, we were making nine hundred.

All but five guys out of the ammunition company that replaced us in the invasion got killed. They called us up to the beachhead, and we set up a supply point there and continued to push on to Rome. From that point on, we supplied the ammunition to the artillery units moving through Italy.

Chief Warrant Officer, U.S. Army

When I got home after the war, I wrote to the National Archives in Washington D.C. to get the information about my unit, and they said it was top secret. I was the commander of an American Legion post at the time, which made it easier to request information from the archives about the modification of the shells.[2] They gave me the information about the amount of ammunition we supplied and told me my unit had received a commendation for manufacturing the shells.

I got discharged in December 1945, and right after I got home a friend of mine talked me into going into the National Guard. The highest rank I could get when I was on private duty was a private first class because there were "no vacancies" for any promotions. I received a master's in education and fought for the hiring of minorities and women for management positions. I had four daughters and one son, and I wanted them to have equal rights, and in order to do that, you have to fight.

---

1 The town of Anzio, Italy—specifically a fifteen-mile-wide beachhead nearby—was the location of an amphibious invasion by Allied troops in early 1944. Landing unopposed and setting up a sizable force, the intent was to immediately strike through the German defensive line and continue into Rome; however, the invasion force, under the command of General John Lucas, delayed their push inland, allowing the German defenders time to recover and surround the Allied force. The result was a four-month struggle that cost thousands of lives on both sides.

2 The American Legion is a veterans organization founded in 1919. They are the nation's largest veterans organization, with over fourteen thousand posts worldwide, and approximately 2.6 million members.

710
SAN

"Nothing to say. It's in the past."

Stanley KARGOL, Private, U.S. Army

Idea Improving Anti-Aircraft Fire Wins City Corporal's Promotion

Sergeant Zilley also gets Furlough and Marries Girl in Florida after Permission by Army

A Philadelphia soldier attached to the Antilles Air Task Force, responsible for the air defense of the Caribbean area, has won commendation from high ranking officers for a suggestion which has resulted in increased effectiveness of anti-aircraft fire.

He is Sergeant Joseph Zilley, 26, of 1736 Green st., now home on furlough after more than a year's service in the Caribbean. His idea, involving a better method of correcting the range of anti-aircraft batteries, has been adopted officially by Caribbean units.

Sergeant Zilley, while serving as a spotter for an anti-aircraft gun crew, noticed that the reverberation of the guns made it difficult to correct the range by the method of telephonic communication then in use.

Colored Lights Used

So he suggested to his superior officer that a system of colored signal lights might be used. These could be flashed on at the gun emplacements by the spotters to show if the bullets were striking above, below, to one side or the other or in the center of the target, he outlined.

He pointed out that a method of this sort might enable the gun crews make necessary adjustments of fire more rapidly than the system. Impressed by Zilley's officers gave him permis-

Sgt. JOSEPH ZILLEY

highly successful. The Coast Artillery command was appraised of it and a letter of commendation promptly followed. With it came Zilley's promotion to his present rank. He had been a corporal.

When he arrived back in the United States recently, Sergeant Zilley wanted to marry the girl he had left behind him, Miss Mary Morris, 1013 Mt. Vernon st. But being officially on overseas service, he had to write to Puerto Rico for Army permission.

This was granted together with an extension of his furlough. So they were married on April 17 in St. James R. C. Church, Orlando, Fla. Sergeant Zilley returns to foreign duty next week.

Zilley (right) with fellow soldier.

Joseph ZILLEY

WHEN THEY DRAFTED ME, I WAS building airplanes at the Rising Sun School of Aeronautics. I was dealing with the construction of an airplane—the ribs, landing support, the wing system. I told the Army all that, but they assigned me to the anti-aircraft—and they stationed me in Puerto Rico! From that moment forward, I was always somewhere other than the front.

It was the 910th Anti-Aircraft Battalion. We had gun positions all around San Juan and spent our time devising different combat tactics. When I arrived, the problem with their anti-aircraft batteries was that they would show the gunner where the plane was by two lines intersecting—but it wouldn't give him the super-elevation, meaning the time flight from the shell to the plane. I devised a sight that contained crosshairs. As the gun moved, the crosshairs would move and show the gunner exactly where he was at that particular moment. Whatever the distance a gun could fire, it would allow the gunner to see that far. If it was a 40mm, it would only go about a mile. If it was used on a five-inch gun, it would go further. They could see from a distance whether those shells were going below or above.

The anti-aircraft guns contained a board that we rigged up with three buttons on it. The two main ones would show the gunner whether he was firing above the target or below the target. If the spotter pushed one button, a green light would light up on the gun and the gunner would know if he was firing too high. If he was shooting too low, a different light would illuminate and he would make a correction.

It was just my nature that I would try to improve things. But I didn't have no mechanical background or anything. I'd toy around with things, and sometimes my experiments would gel. Wherever there was a problem, I'd try to lick it!

I came up with another idea that would have saved the government a lot of money and improve the efficiency of the anti-aircraft guns. These guns sat on a big platform, and to move them around, there were a bunch of parts: a power plant, cables, and a director. And we would have to haul these things around. But there was enough room on the platform for one Briggs and Stratton motor, and that would have produced enough power to move the gun around laterally and vertically, and we could have eliminated the other parts. But some manufacturers sold the government on the idea that they needed those parts.

Even if the soldiers had good ideas, the businesses controlled how far we got with combat tactics and technological improvements.

Technician Fourth Grade, U.S. Army

"I wanted to get into the Army, which was so stupid. I didn't realize how dangerous it was. It just looked so glamorous. All my friends were in uniform looking heroic, and there I was walking around in a suit and tie. I went to the draft board and I said, 'Put my name down.' So they did, and I got drafted. I was put in this Army Specialized Training Program. My mother, if she had ever known—she would have killed me."

— Sumner Jules GLIMCHER

Sumner Jules GLIMCHER

MY MOST MEMORABLE NIGHT STARTed when I got shot at five o'clock in the afternoon. It was Christmas Day and we were in the Ardennes Forest. This was during the Battle of the Bulge.[1] We climbed up a hill, ran into a clearing, and faced a barrage of gunfire, shellfire, rifles, machine guns. You can tell by the way the shell whistles if it's going to hit you or go over your head. When I heard my shell, I knew. It just had my name on it. I felt a weight on my leg, and a soldier pulled me back behind a rock with these two other injured guys. Then the battle moved ahead. We could hear the sounds of the guns disappear. The two other guys were unconscious. When the captain left us, he said, "I'm going to call the medics and give them your location." As far as I knew, there wasn't a soul within miles. As I passed out, I thought we were going to bleed to death. Luckily it was so cold the blood froze. I woke up seven hours later to this noise and grabbed my gun. The moon was bright and I saw these two American medics with a stretcher come into the clearing—it was truly a miracle.

They drove us to a field hospital and operated on me. They gave me sodium pentothal, which is an anesthetic. And it's a wonderful anesthetic. Absolutely great. I woke up in a tent to all these beautiful nurses. I thought it was a dream.

When I was put into a hospital bed, I found out I had frostbite. The pain was immense as the blood began to try to circulate through my capillaries, which had frozen stiff. The docs told me that I might have to have my toes amputated. They sent me to a hospital in Wales, and the chief of staff there told me they were going to amputate my leg! My whole leg was infected, and I was in danger of getting gangrene. Then he told me the Brits had just discovered a new antibiotic. Would I like to try it out? I said, "God, let's try it out!" It was penicillin![2] Every four hours, a nurse would come and stick a needle in my ass, and two weeks later the infection cleared out. So it was more like three miracles: I didn't die, I didn't lose my toes, and I didn't lose my leg.

I *wanted* to get into the Army, which was so stupid. I didn't realize how dangerous it was. It just looked so glamorous. All my friends were in uniform looking heroic, and there I was walking around in a suit and tie. I went to the draft board and I said, "Put my name down." So they did, and I got drafted. I was put in this Army Specialized Training Program.[3] My mother, if she had ever known, she would have killed me.

After seeing the first dead American soldier in Europe, I couldn't fire my rifle. I don't remember if I lifted up my rifle and pretended to shoot or not, but I didn't believe in killing people. I did not want to contribute to anybody's death, even the enemy's. Because they were people like us. I suppose I wouldn't have had a problem shooting Hitler. If he were in front of me and somebody gave me a gun and said "Shoot him!" I would have done it in a minute.

While I was still in combat, another soldier and I came across a German prisoner. He was a young kid, probably only about twelve years old. This guy I was with had just lost his best buddy to a sniper the previous day. Theoretically, you're supposed to take a prisoner and bring him back. When he saw this kid, he took his gun and he began to beat him. His rifle butt was a big heavy thing, and the boy began to cry. He beat this kid until he died. I couldn't stand that. It still upsets me when I think about it today.

When the war was over and I had healed, I saw a big headline in *Stars and Stripes* that said the military government needed German-speaking interpreters. I had studied three years of high-school German, so I had some basic knowledge. I reported to Paris and told them I spoke German. I was afraid they would give me a test, but they didn't, and, on top of it all, I had this terrific weekend with a lovely young lady in Paris. I met her in the Folies Bergére—it was a live burlesque show and it was the sexiest thing you'd ever seen. French girls parading around, and they started taking off their clothes. I was an innocent kid way up in the balcony in the cheap seats, and down there in the front row were all the baldheaded generals: Eisenhower, Patton. When the show ended, I walked out and somebody grabbed my arm. It was one of the ladies of the night that hung out by the

Private First Class, U.S. Army

Sumner Glimcher (right) in Bavaria, 1945.

theater because they knew all these American soldiers would be ready for sex and perfect company to pick up. She took me to a hotel and we spent two days there, until suddenly I realized I was AWOL. I could go to prison for that! I was supposed to have been back Sunday night and here it was Tuesday. I gave her all the chocolate and cigarettes I had—in those days, cigarettes and chocolate bars were currency. Later, I bought a Leica camera for six packs of cigarettes!

The Germans were docile, friendly, and very accommodating. I began my work as an interpreter with all kinds of civilians. I became an investigator because we had to appoint people to jobs who were politically neutral, who had not been ardent Nazis. Anybody who applied for a job had to fill out a questionnaire, and we asked questions like, "When did you join the Nazi party?" If they joined in 1933 when Hitler really took power, they were an ardent Nazis. If they joined in the late twenties, they were Nazis before Hitler even came into power. People who joined in 1939 were low on the Nazi scale. The Germans answered very honestly. They would write down what rank they'd held, and if they were awarded any decorations. They would put everything down meticulously. Based on that, I could weed out who were Nazis and we wouldn't appoint them as a mayor or a police chief.

You think of nations having certain characteristics, like the Italians are artists and crazy about opera, music, and food. The French are wild about sex, the English are straight-laced, and, well, the Germans are very meticulous. They're methodical. That's the way they are. That was their nature, to be very honest, and they were cutting their own throats when they were doing it.

---

1 Taking place between December 1944 and January 1945, the Battle of the Bulge was the last major German offensive against Allied forces in World War II. Seeking to prevent the advance of the Allied line into Germany, Hitler ordered his commanders to launch an attack in the Ardennes region of Belgium, Luxembourg, and France. Despite initial success in driving the Allied line back (the "bulge"), a lack of resources prevented German forces from going farther. The largest battle fought by American troops, the casualties numbered over eighty thousand, with approximately nineteen thousand American soldiers killed.

2 Discovered by Alexander Fleming in 1928, the antibiotic penicillin played an incredibly important role in wartime medicine, significantly increasing the chances of survival for those wounded in combat. It was particularly effective against gangrene.

3 Established in 1942, the Army Specialized Training Program was designed to identify and train academically inclined soldiers in skills such as engineering, language, and medicine.

Opposite: **George KOLKA, First Sergeant, U.S. Army** Above: **Sol SEGALL, Technician Third Grade, U.S. Army**

Marian Johnson (back row, 3rd from right) attending a strategy meeting at the WAVES recruiting office in Cleveland, OH.

Marian JOHNSON

Specialist First Class, U.S. Navy (WAVES)

WE WERE VERY ANXIOUS TO GET healthy twenty-year-old girls. The idea was to replace a man from his desk so he could go to war. It was not like nowadays, where the women sign up and march onto the battleships. This was the start of women in the service.

All my friends got involved. The men were all going off to war and we'd sit by the radio, listening. Some gals had husbands who were overseas, and so we were glued to the news about the invasion. It sounded horrible and, consequently, you wanted to help.

In June 1942, I reported for duty at Hunter College. In those days you were sent to Hunter for four weeks of training, and then they would assign you to various parts of the country. I had hoped to be a control tower operator, but they decided I would be better in recruiting duty. I was kind of young, with no experience. I was happy to be assigned near my family in Cleveland, Ohio.

We had a crew. Sometimes it was a crew of six, and sometimes it was just two of us. My commanding officer was Lieutenant Elizabeth Landis-Cullen. She was only about thirty years old. We were based in the Naval Office of Procurement in Cleveland, but we traveled into different towns for week-long stints. We obtained graduation addresses for girls from their high schools and we would call them at home. I would start the conversation by saying, "You have been selected for training in the U.S. Navy!" Then we held interviews from six in the morning to nine at night. We'd ask them about their interests in life, but, of course, we did most of the talking. It was a selling job, strictly.

We didn't accept everybody—there were various reasons to turn someone down. They may have had a baby or were dealing with health issues. We talked to a lot of parents—none objected to the cause. Showing the girls movies usually did the trick, not that it took much to convince them to join. This was not an era of hesitation.

---

1 WAVES was an acronym for Women Accepted for Volunteer Emergency Service. Established in 1942, the organization represented the first time since World War I that the U.S. Navy accepted a significant number of women into their ranks. Further, it was the first time women were able to achieve formal officer status, and occupations were far-ranging, including intelligence, communications, medical, and technical posts.

U.S NAVY

Above: **Jeanne FOX WOOD, First Lieutenant, U.S. Army Nurse Corps** Opposite: **Kathy O'GRADY, U.S. Navy (WAVES)**

CHASE-
STATLER

MY FRIENDS KEPT TEASING ME about joining the Reserves and fulfilling my patriotic duty. I told them that when they open up the Marines to women I would join, considering they were the best. Sure enough, they did, and immediately on approval I found myself with the second class of trainees at Hunter College boot camp, before moving to headquarters in Washington, DC. We were housed at the Cairo Hotel while the barracks near our headquarters, next to Arlington Cemetery, were being finished. After a few temporary assignments I replaced a male Marine as the assistant in charge of the personnel mailroom. Shortly after that I was placed in charge, overseeing three sections and about thirty male and female civilians and Marine personnel. It was challenging at times to prove to the Marine men that we could do the job. Some tried to browbeat us into saying we couldn't do it, but we showed our spunk and everything went well.

There were times when my authority was challenged. I was in charge of a staff sergeant who was a former New York cop. He challenged me on his yearly report, and my supervisor had to put him in his place. Once I had an employee who was up for a promotion but she didn't get it. I had to go the major in charge of our group and tell him that she did the work and deserved it. It put my position at risk, but she got the promotion. No one knew of the many tears of great satisfaction in the ladies room after such incidents. After all is said and done it makes me proud to have served as a Marine.

Technical Sergeant, U.S. Marine Corps

I HAD LOST A VERY GOOD FRIEND AT the beginning of the war. He had been my next-door neighbor, and I was very fond of him. I thought that it would be a nice thing to join the Navy as he had done. I joined the Women Accepted for Volunteer Emergency Service.[1] We were called "ninety-day wonders," because they trained us in ninety days. But at this particular time, they were so eager to get us onboard that they cut two weeks off the training.

There were about eighty thousand WAVES, and out of that number ten percent were officers, and I happened to be one of them. I felt very fortunate. At one point, I got to board the *Sequoia*, which was the presidential yacht during the war. It was docked in the Potomac River at the Navy Yard. We went onboard the ship and we got to see the state room where Roosevelt slept—he had a wooden wheelchair by the bed. At the end of the tour, they sat us up on the deck and gave us cookies and iced tea in gold-rimmed glasses. I'll never forget that. Everything looked, felt, smelled, and tasted so important during those days.

Lieutenant, U.S. Navy (WAVES)

1 See pg. 92, footnote 1.

"One of the reasons that the Tuskegee Airman organization was started was to let the world know that there were black pilots fighting in World War II. When we got back here, nobody believed it had actually happened. It's not like the newspapers or radios talked about it. If you looked at history books or anything official, you didn't see it. There was nothing that you could point to."

— Ted LUMPKIN

Ted LUMPKIN

THE DRAFT BOARD SENT ALL LOS Angeles draftees to Fort MacArthur to be inducted into the service. Three of us assigned to Tuskegee were put on a civilian train and assigned to a specific compartment.[1] One fellow had been studying and following up on Tuskegee for a while. Listening to him, I started getting really impressed with how wonderful an assignment this was going to be. But when we got to the Mason-Dixon Line, we found out why we were in the compartment. We were restricted to that compartment. All of us were black and were familiar with a certain kind of treatment, but this was our first brush with an official kind of prejudice that we hadn't encountered before.

The train let us off in Chehaw, Alabama. It was a rainy, muddy day. We all thought that we were at the wrong place. There was nothing except trees and a dirt road. They sent a truck for us, and we went on into Tuskegee. There was a lot of construction and big heavy equipment there. They were building the field at the time, and it was really quite impressive.

After some very difficult basic training, I was assigned to an administrative position. That's where I discovered that I could apply for officers school. I took an exam and got accepted and went down to Miami Beach, Florida. The Air Force had taken over all these resorts and used them to house all of the personnel. Punch was my roommate, Vernon Punch. He was the epitome of a military guy. He'd had a lot of previous experience. He had a girlfriend, Peaches. I always remember Peaches when I think of or see a peach. He was so crazy about her, and that's all he could talk about. Our class in itself included five thousand people. Seventeen out of five thousand men in officers training for the U.S. Air Force were black. The experience was good there. The classes were integrated. When we finished the course, all seventeen of us were then assigned to Tuskegee, and to the 100th Fighter Squadron, 332nd Fighter Group.

Ted Lumpkin at Ramitelli Airfield, Italy, counting fighter planes returning from a combat mission.

We were sent overseas to Italy, where I had an intelligence officer assignment. Our squadron was assigned to the Fifteenth Air Force, which focused on strategic, military targets. At that point, our mission basically changed to escorting bombers to their various targets in northern Italy and the eastern part of Europe. We particularly focused on the oil fields to prevent the Germans from getting oil.

Our planes faced a great deal of anti-aircraft fire, which was very effective and probably gave us more trouble than enemy fighters. Colonel Benjamin O. Davis, our commander, really insisted on the planes escorting the bombers and not getting distracted by the enemy fighters. Most of the pilots didn't like that restriction. They preferred to engage in dogfights and show how good they were. Some of the pilots were pretty feisty about that because they wanted to be aces. The rest of the Air Force had their aces. We were being held back in order to show that the blacks weren't good enough to fight. It was upsetting, but we overcame that and, ultimately, it proved to be the thing our whole reputation was built on—the ability to stay with those bombers and to protect them from the enemy fighters. We had an excellent record in comparison to other fighter groups.

The 332nd was good at protecting bombers, but the loss of our own pilots was a very emotional thing. It is difficult to accept the "here today and gone tomorrow" element of war. For example, 100th Commander Robert Tressville, a West Point graduate, had a bright future

Ted Lumpkin (bottom left) and fellow Tuskegee Airmen at Ramitelli Airfield, Italy.

in our organization. In Italy, he devised a mission to go behind the enemy lines without our fighters being detected by the German radar. In order to do so, they had to fly real low. Four pilots were included in this mission, and Jefferson, his wingman, was a real good friend of mine. They were flying so low that they got to the point where the horizon and the water come together. They didn't make it; their planes evidently flew straight into the water.

But bad times were balanced out with good. One major mission was a long-distance one to Berlin. The fighters had to carry extra gasoline tanks in order to escort the bombers to the target and back. The mission was kind of critical. It was one of the few times that the Eighth Air Force and the Fifteenth Air Force coordinated to help knock the Germans out of the war. It was a hazardous mission, because the Germans were defending their capital as strongly as they could. But we succeeded, and it felt really good to be part of such a major moment in the war.

One time B-24 bombers had to land on our base due to bad weather. This was the first time that they discovered the Redtails were black pilots.[2] They knew that Redtail planes would stay with their bombers, but they didn't know that black pilots were flying them. They had all ranges of reaction—from surprise to "Oh, you're just another person like I am" to a crew that would not even get out of their bomber because they didn't want to be housed with black troops.

On the base we didn't experience prejudice, because we were an all-black organization. We felt that in the first part of the war, there were a lot of stories being told by white American troops regarding black troops: that they had tails, that they were different from white troops. It was kind of hearsay, whether these things were actually said or not. We could only prove that based on the Italians asking us if it were true. As the Italians got to know us better, we got to know them better and the relationship between our troops was very good. I enjoyed our experience in Italy because you were looked at and judged as a person.

That's why it was a little disappointing when we got back to the States, where you were black first, and then they looked at other things you might have done. One of the reasons that the Tuskegee Airman organization was started was to let the world know that there were black pilots fighting in World War II. When we got back, nobody believed it had actually happened. It's not like the newspapers or radios talked about our experience. If you looked at history books or anything official, there was nothing that you could point to. It's not that people didn't believe you; it's just that they didn't see it confirmed or discussed anywhere. That had a dampening effect. It wasn't really until around 1972 that the Tuskegee organization formed to promote the legacy and formally asked people to do what they could to spread the word.

We received the Congressional Gold Medal in 2007, and President Bush saluted the Tuskegee Airmen for the many salutes that they had not received during their active duty. Often, a white enlisted person did not salute a black officer. The big salute from the president symbolized all of the missed ones.

---

1 America's first black military aviators were trained at Tuskegee Army Airfield in Alabama, which provided the origin of their popular title: the Tuskegee Airmen.

2 The Tuskegee Airmen painted the tails of their aircraft a distinctive red to identify themselves, earning them the nickname "Redtails" or "Red Tail Angels."

First Lieutenant, U.S. Air Force

Opposite: **Jerry ZUK, Private First Class, U.S. Army** Above: **Paul BLAIR, Staff Sergeant, U.S. Army**

"I signed up for what they called a three-year hitch. This was a month before Pearl Harbor. After December 7th, you were in for what they called the duration."

— Louis "Larry" SILBERLING

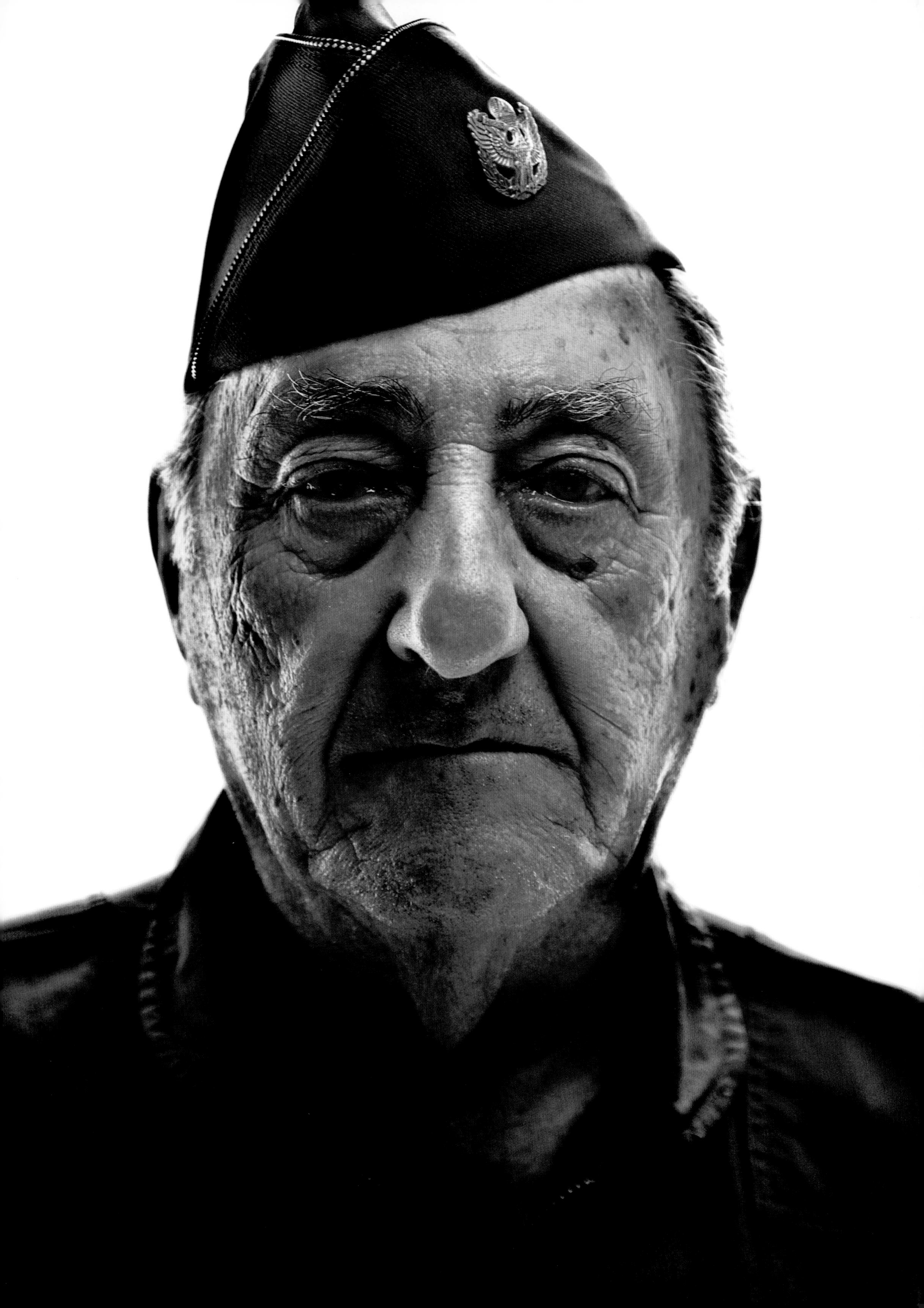

Louis "Larry" SILBERLING

I WOULD WATCH THE PLANES TAKE off at the Floyd Bennett Field in Brooklyn and dream about becoming a pilot. You had to be twenty-one to join the Air Corps, but my father signed me up because he had just married a highfalutin woman and was ready to get rid of me. At the recruiting office, the old sergeant was calling out, "Louis! Louis, come up here!" I wasn't paying attention to him. I didn't know who Louis was. Finally he came over to me and said, "Didn't you hear me call you?" I said, "Not me. My name is Lawrence. My friends call me Larry." That made him mad. "Oh, is that right?" He took me by the tie and he pulled me up to the front of the room. He put my head down on his desk and there was my birth certificate: Louis Silberling. Never knew it until I joined the Army! I signed up for what they called a three-year hitch. This was a month before Pearl Harbor. After December 7th, you were in for what they called the duration.

They were losing a lot of gunners on these bombers in Europe. Boy, they were getting shot down fast. They needed new ones badly, but you had to volunteer for it. So I took the test and I passed. They sent me to aerial gunnery school in Panama City. With Clark Gable! I used to go out with him at night because women were crazy for him. I figured, what can I lose? If I go with him, I get his overflow!

Brigadier General William Albert Matheny awarding Silberling an oak leaf cluster.

We started flying out of Miami to shoot down German submarines that were coming up too close to us. The disadvantage was that we used the Miami airport, which was half civilian, half military. We flew out with old pre-war airplanes that weren't worth a damn. Old bombers. Undermanned as far as machine guns and all that, .30 calibers instead of .50 calibers.

They put radar aboard, which was new at the time, and sent us to Trinidad, Cuba, and the Dutch Indies. The submarines surfaced at night because they had to be on top of the water to charge their batteries. That's when we went looking for them. We'd find them, but couldn't get anywhere near them. They had good deck guns on them. Good gunners. They would knock these B-18s out of the sky like nothing.[1] We couldn't approach them with our little .30 caliber machine guns. Finally the Navy got smart and gave us B-24 Liberators.[2] That's when we started to do some good. If we dropped depth charges from within seventeen feet, on either side of the hull, we would blow their seams and sink them.

One day on the field this guy comes over and tells me, "If I fly for you tonight, and you fly for me tomorrow night, I can keep this date with a cute Dutch girl I met in town." So we talked to the captain and he okayed the switch. He flew for me that night, and they never came back. Him, my whole crew, and the airplane. Nobody came back. They went down, obviously, but how we don't know.

Our first real base was in Guadalcanal. The crew camping next to us were called "short-timers," which meant they were practically finished with their stretch of duty and were almost ready to go home. As it was, we were scared, we didn't know what the hell to expect. I thought, "Geez, I'd like to talk to these guys." We wanted to get the scoop on the aerial combat out there. So we all went over to their tent after dinner one night and they answered all of our questions. The next afternoon, we were in our tents filling out paperwork and a truck pulls up alongside the short-timers' tent. Some guys get out and start taking all the stuff out of the tent and loading it on the truck. I said, "What are you doing? What's happening?" He said, "This crew didn't make it—they never came back." Those guys were so nice, and ready to go home—it was one of the saddest moments for me. We hadn't even had our first real mission yet.

Sometimes when you were up in the air, the anti-aircraft fire was so thick and numerous, you felt like you

Technical Sergeant, U.S. Air Force

Louis Silberling (far right) and fellow soldiers stand atop a B-24 Liberator while stationed on the island of Curacao.

could get out and walk on those black puffs. But they were shrapnel, and the steel would go right through our planes. The fuel was in the wings, and if shrapnel hit those, it would blow the plane up. The worst mission was in Borneo—the Battle of Balikpapan.[3] They gave us a briefing in a big open tent. When a priest gave us last rites, I said, "Oh boy." I knew we were in trouble right there and then.

The Balikpapan oil fields were the blood of the Japanese air force and trucks. It took eight and a half hours for us to get there over water. Our fighters couldn't go that far, so we had no protection. A lot of planes got shot down, but we made it to the other side of the island. We weren't dealing with the original Japanese fighters we fought in the early part of the war, they were good pilots. Instead it was these guys who would stop at nothing—if they didn't shoot you down, they collided right into you. A lot of our guys didn't come back. But we survived it—all seventeen hours in the air.

1 Designed in 1935 to replace the B-10 as the U.S. Army Air Corps' standard bomber, the underpowered B-18 was swiftly rotated out of active service after the bombing of Pearl Harbor, and reassigned to transport or modified for anti-submarine duties.

2 The B-24 Liberator was an American heavy bomber developed in 1939. The B-24 had a long range and high top speed, and had great success in operations in the Pacific, European, and African Theaters. More than eighteen thousand were produced, the largest quantity of aircraft built during the Second World War.

3 Balikpapan, in southeast Borneo, was the location of an oil refinery of strategic importance to the Japanese forces, providing oil, aviation fuel, and petroleum. Following a battle with Allied forces in 1942, the Japanese remained in control of the area. In 1944, heavy bombers under the command of General St. Clair Street demolished the refinery, and Allied forces captured the area in 1945, concluding the Borneo campaign.

Above: **Willis LOEHR, Colonel, U.S. Air Force** Opposite: **Jewell PHELPS, Sergeant, U.S. Army**

"When we joined the WASPs we were promised militarization, but ugly politics took over. Walter Winchell, Drew Pearson, and a lot of commentators decided that women should not fly in their valuable military aircraft."

— Edna Modisette DAVIS

Edna Modisette DAVIS

After World War I, my father bought an old, open cockpit airplane, the famous Jenny. I was six, and we flew for fun for a year when he crashed the plane softly into lake Erie. Shortly thereafter, we moved to Santa Monica and I took my love for flying with me. I saved my allowance, nickel by nickel and dime by dime, so that when I reached a dollar I could ride in an old circus plane for fifteen minutes.

I was attending the University of California at Berkeley when World War II broke out. Due to the shortage of male pilots to fight the war, the government offered the Civilian Pilot Training program. When I went to sign up, they said, "No, you're a girl." My answer was, "I'm a girl, but I want to do it anyway." After several weeks of daily insistence, I was invited to attend the training class given at Mills College, a progressive women's college in nearby Oakland. I received my private pilot's license flying out of Oakland Airport.

At this time, General Arnold was formulating the WASPs—the Women Airforce Service Pilots—under the direction of Jacquelin Cochran in Texas.[1] I flew, studied, and managed to graduate six months early and took off for Ft. Worth to sign up. Fortunately I was able to meet with Jackie and was completely dazzled by her. Her first words to me were, "You are too skinny. I will give you a week—you eat, get fat and I'll send the orders for your physical." So I rented a room and ate and ate and ate, and I hate to eat. Still short two pounds for the requirements, I saw the kindly sergeant push the scale forward and he passed me. Next came the long train ride to Sweetwater, Texas, to join the first class of women to train in military aircraft at Avenger Field.[2]

We were each given two pairs of used overalls as uniforms. They were made for men over six feet tall and two hundred pounds. In order to keep them on we had to tie a belt tight around our waists and roll up the legs and sleeves. We had male trainees on base for three weeks until someone decided that was not a good combination. Hence, only women took Primary, Basic, and Advanced training on Avenger Field. At every opportunity I let the world know that I wanted to fly the B-26 Martin Marauder, so when I graduated I was chosen to go with an experimental group of women to train in Dodge City, Kansas.[3]

It was bleak, cold, and snowy in Dodge. We lived in tar-paper barracks with German prisoners of war as orderlies. We first flew the infamous "short wing" that had earned the nickname the "Widow Maker." The planes had a bad reputation from the start. Women were really sent to Dodge to embarrass the men and to prove that the B-26 was safe and beautiful to fly.

I was the first woman to be certified in the left seat (1st. Pilot), but when I went for my final check ride there was no crew, just an empty airplane. After the commander of the base threatened a court marshal, the crew arrived and eventually agreed to stay and transfer with us to our final assignments. Eleven of us graduated and proved that women could fly anything in the Air Force fleet.

My job then was to fly the B-26, towing a large mesh target for the training of gunners in B-24s. The gunners were given different colored bullets in each of their .50 caliber machine guns to identify their accuracy.

When we joined the WASPs we were promised militarization, but ugly politics took over. Walter Winchell, Drew Pearson, and a lot of commentators decided that women should not fly in their valuable military aircraft.

Edna Davis in the cockpit of a B-26 Marauder.

Captain, U.S. Air Force (WASP)

WASPs marching at Avenger Field in Sweetwater, Texas.

The Tuskegee airmen were having the same trouble for being black. But they were militarized; we were just civil servants.

We were sabotaged—sugar put in the gas tank, wires cut—but without fatalities as far as I know. When you are seven women flying on an airbase of thirty-seven thousand men, you just do your job and everything is fine. When one of our pilots was killed, we WASPs collected our money to send our gal home to be buried. Her family was not allowed to put the gold star in their window, which was the tradition when a pilot or soldier died.

When the men started returning towards the end of war, they sent us home. We had three weeks to leave our base, find our own way home by bus or car; no monies, no thank you.

In 1977, Congress finally passed a bill incorporating us into the military. Though no benefits were given, other than VA hospital care and burial. Then, in 2010, all WASPs, living or dead, received the highest honor Congress can bestow upon a civilian, the Congressional Gold Medal. It took sixty-five years. We are all proud and glad we were a part of history, and helped pave the way for future female pilots.

Looking back we had to face the fact that men had it much easier. Have you ever wondered what in the world women did when they needed to relieve themselves while flying? Men had the "relief tube." On one freezing night flying over North Dakota we were all bundled up in heavy fleece-lined togs and boots. I took two Dixie cups and walked back to the rear of the plane and very carefully managed to fill them. As I walked slowly back to the front to pour them into the relief tube, the pilots and crew, who were all laughing hard, opened the bomb bay doors as I crossed the twelve-inch cat walk. I'm standing there, looking down at the snow-covered earth, and I just turned my cups upside down and said, "Bombs away!"

---

1 A pioneering American aviator, Jaqueline Cochran was an accomplished racing pilot before World War II. After training with the Royal Air Force in Britain, Cochran spearheaded the effort to train female pilots in the U.S. military, and she served as the director of the Women Airforce Service Pilots.

2 Opened in 1941, Avenger Field was an airfield used as a training base by the U.S. military. It is particularly notable as the location where the WASPs trained, becoming an all-female base in 1943.

3 A twin-engined medium bomber, the Martin B-26 Marauder was a fast aircraft with a small wing area, deployed primarily in Europe, along with the Mediterranean and Pacific Theaters. Early models had a high rate of accidents due to the unique design, high performance, and lack of experienced pilots and mechanics.

Jim WHITE

When I was a kid, I won this contest out of a Hollywood newspaper and my prize was a trip in the old Goodyear Blimp. That was my first time off the ground. I was a senior in high school when I took the test to become an aviation cadet. I went into preflight training two weeks after I graduated; a little over a year later I got my wings.

I wanted to fly fighter planes, but at the time, all they needed were bomber pilots. They shipped us out to Nebraska to pick up the brand new B-17 right out of the factory.[1] We had to calibrate the air speed, altimeters, and all of the basic instruments on the airplane while we were there.

On our way to Europe, we flew to Goose Bay in Canada, where the Army had a small airbase. Marlene Dietrich happened to be there at the officers club that night. She'd immigrated to the U.S. before the war and was not sympathetic to the German cause. I was only twenty, and boy, what an impression she made on me! I can still see her sitting on that baby grand piano. She had her black dress on, split up the side to her hip—it was sexy.

Jim White in uniform, 1945.

I was assigned to the 398th Bombardment Group, part of the 1st Air Division. We flew bombing runs all over Germany: Cologne, Marsberg, Berlin. My eighteenth mission, on Christmas Eve, December 24th 1944, was during the Battle of the Bulge. It was going to be a very easy mission, a milk run with very little flak expected to be shooting at us. The weather was horrible, and there was ice on the plane that they couldn't get off. But this mission was what was called "a maximum effort," which meant you flew almost regardless of any problems with the airplane.

On top of that, we were assigned to a base that had a very short runway for heavy bombers. We couldn't clear

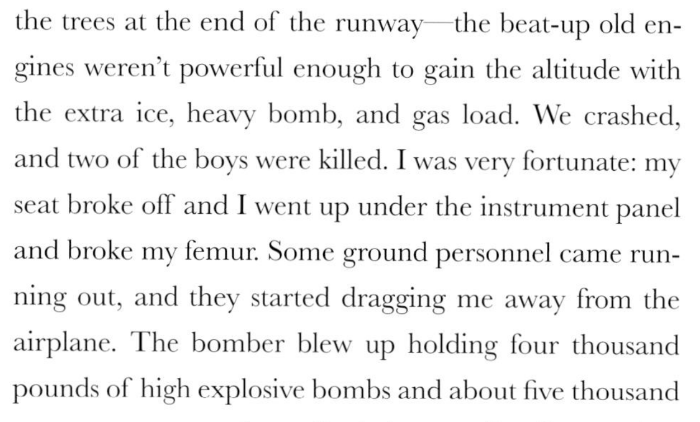

the trees at the end of the runway—the beat-up old engines weren't powerful enough to gain the altitude with the extra ice, heavy bomb, and gas load. We crashed, and two of the boys were killed. I was very fortunate: my seat broke off and I went up under the instrument panel and broke my femur. Some ground personnel came running out, and they started dragging me away from the airplane. The bomber blew up holding four thousand pounds of high explosive bombs and about five thousand gallons of aviation gasoline. I remember just fatalistically putting my hands over my eyes, thinking that was it.

I ended up in the hospital in England from Christmas Eve until Easter. They shipped me home in a body cast from my neck to my toes. I was a slab. All I could move were my toes and my arms. They took me home to New York on the *Queen Elizabeth*; we had to zigzag all the way with no escort.[2] They had me down on the bottom deck, because if something had gone wrong, I would've been in the way in my cast. It would have taken at least two guys to lift me.

It was raining the night we arrived in New York, and they had German POWs unloading the immobile veterans. I was going down the gangplank on my back, rain on my face, looking up at the chin of a German prisoner who hadn't shaved in a week. He was grubby and didn't speak any English. All of a sudden I wondered, is he going to dump me in? I would have gone down like a brick. But he kindly pulled the blanket up over my face to keep the rain out instead.

First Lieutenant, U.S. Army Air Corps

---

1 A four-engine heavy bomber, the B-17 Flying Fortress was used in strategic bombing campaigns, primarily against German industrial and military targets.

2 The RMS *Queen Elizabeth* was an ocean liner, the largest passenger ship of its time, constructed in the 1930s and converted into a troopship during the Second World War.

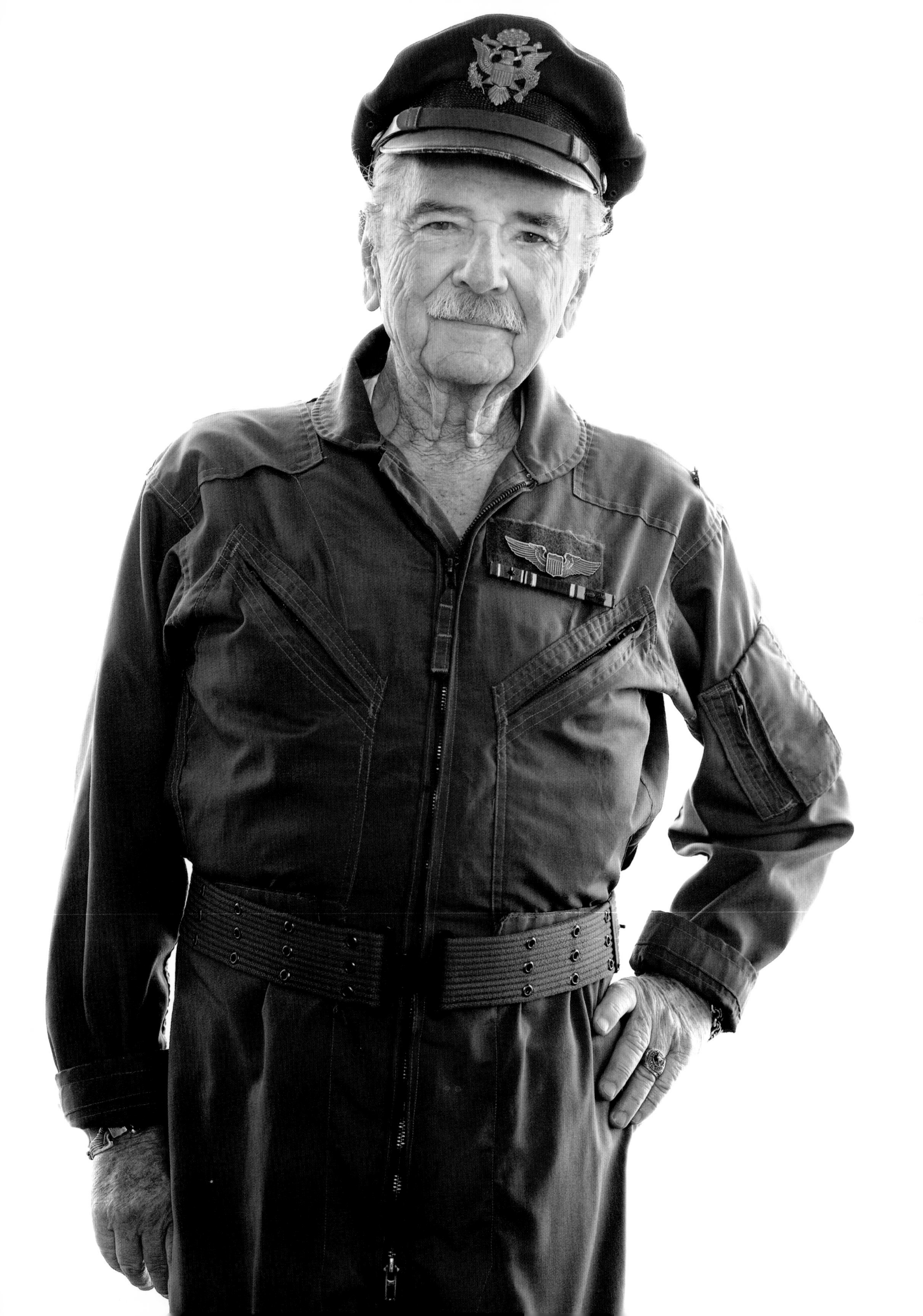

Above: **William SCROGGINS, Sergeant First Class, U.S. Army** Opposite: **Edmond ACKERMAN, Seaman First Class, U.S. Navy**

21 73701

I GREW UP IN A FAMILY OF SINGERS. When I graduated from Hollywood High, I was chosen to sing a Victor Herbert song at the Hollywood Bowl. I worked in nightclubs during and after high school. I sang in Vegas back when it only had two hotels. To get the jobs, you had to sing both popular and classical songs because you never knew what would be requested. Even before I went overseas to entertain the boys, I was traveling everywhere. But the thing I loved most in my performing days was singing for the soldiers. Oh, there's nothing like it.

There were about ten people in my USO crew—singers, dancers, a comedian, a master of ceremonies.[1] We couldn't wear dresses when we were overseas; we had to wear uniforms, very nice jackets and pants. At night we put on the glamorous stuff. I remember singing the song "Embraceable You" because the sailors requested it all the time. Sometimes we performed for five hundred people, sometimes we played for a group of ten. Once I sang and played the ukulele for two soldiers guarding a bridge.

Frank Adagio was an adorable dancer in my crew. He was very talented, and all the women loved dancing with him. He was quite short, however, and sometimes men who were six feet tall would come over while we were dancing and say, "May I have this dance?" But I fell madly in love with him, and we ended up married for sixty years.

We were stationed in the Moana Hotel in Hawaii for five months before we started traveling the islands in the Pacific. I was never homesick, and I loved every moment. There was only one time when I got scared, and that was in Guam. A siren went off and we were driven up a hill to an air shelter. It ended up being a hurricane, and we stayed in the shelter with all the navy guys for three days—food rationing, cots, the whole experience. I felt like one of the boys.

Studio portrait of Angel Adagio.

It wasn't just sing-y and it wasn't just dance-y—real stuff was going on. We performed in hospitals, sometimes where the boys were badly hurt. Someone once cried while I was singing pretty—that was hard to take. But I just had to remember that I was doing something good. One time a soldier came up to me with his head all wrapped up and said, "I'm President Truman." The hospital staff had told us, "Whatever they tell you, believe it." So we all said, "Oh, we're very happy to know you, President Truman." Every time we ran into him, we said, "How are you, Mr. President?"

Performer, USO

Another time a young soldier came over to me and said, "You know, I really liked the way you sing. I'd like to give you a million-dollar contract." I said, "I'm so pleased that you like me, but I already have an agent." That's one thing I never forget. There were a lot of terrible things going on, but there was a surprising amount of humor.

Flyer featuring Angel Adagio (left) using her stage name, Lucile Angel.

1 The United Service Organizations (USO) is a nonprofit group established in 1941 with the purpose of providing morale, welfare, and recreation services to U.S. military personnel.

Robert COSTA

Fireman, U.S. Navy

Robert Costa in uniform, 1944.

TODAY ALL THEY HAVE TO DO IS put in a disc and it's over. I had to haul two big projectors around the ship, climb up ladders, and hang a great big canvas sheet from gun turrets. I was known as "special effects," but they had to put me somewhere so they gave me the fireman title. But I was pretty independent as far as duties go. All I had to do was show the movies.

My timing was perfect. I went to boot camp at Naval Station Great Lakes. The projectionist at the Navy Pier in Chicago broke his hand in a fight and couldn't do it anymore. On my record, they could see that I had worked in a film library as a teenager. It was just a continuation of showing movies, but now it was 35mm instead of 16mm. I had that for about a year, and it was really great. But then I was sent to Pearl Harbor, to serve on the newly repaired and re-commissioned *Nevada* and shipped out to Pearl Harbor.[1] I was on a train to Los Angeles when they announced that Japan had surrendered. Boy, was I glad to hear that.

At the Navy Pier in Chicago, we used to get the movies before they were released to the public. But aboard ship, you had to stock up. In those days, everything was physical. When you traded films, you ran a line to a ship in the middle of the ocean. There was nothing but water everywhere as you watched your film swing across the sea over to them, and vice versa. That's the way it was done.

The guys didn't like war films—it's just like if you're depressed about something, you don't want to watch a heavy movie, you want to watch something that will make you forget, that will make you laugh. They loved *The Three Caballeros*, the Disney film about South America with Donald Duck. See, anything with music lightened their hearts. Once we hadn't made a rendezvous with any ships for a while, so all I had was a Popeye cartoon. Every night that's what I put on, until one night, I saw the guys climbing up the gun turret. They wanted to kill me! "If you show that cartoon one more time…!"

It was a natural talent. I just loved it. I ended up in Hollywood right after the war. It took a while, but I created a production company in Los Angeles and we worked on shows like *That Was the Week That Was* and *The Red Skelton Show*. Eventually I did production and special effects for *Terminator 2*, *Starman*, *History of the World*, *Robocop*, and *Superman*. It was really something. The Navy literally changed my life. It was on that ship when I realized the effect film has on people.

The ships used to dump films over the side when they wanted to get rid of them. Well, I liberated some of that. I didn't know what I was picking up but thought, "Well, maybe there's something interesting here." There was one film reel I brought home that was very different than anything I'd seen on the screen. It was footage of a kamikaze plane hitting the chief's quarters of a ship. Someone captured it on film. Men lying on deck, blood all over the place. It was the footage that the public never sees. The newsreels are always, "Oh we're doing so well, and we've advanced so far!" We can't know what the reality of something is unless we experience it, or unless someone who is really wonderful at conveying things can tell us. But even then you still don't *really* see it.

---

1 The USS *Nevada* was launched in 1914 and served in both World Wars. The only battleship to get under way during the December 7, 1941 attack on Pearl Harbor, the *Nevada* suffered significant damage before being repaired and returned to duty.

“I do not watch war pictures or talk war. It is hell.”

George NILAN, Sergeant, U.S. Army

108
CALIFO

I REALLY WAS NOT A VERY SEXY soldier. I lived in Chicago when I got drafted. They found out I was a psychologist and asked me if I wanted to go to Officer Candidate School. If I went, I would have to be in the Army for a set number of years. I said, "Hell no." See, I'm a coward. Not a bad coward, a good one. I certainly thought that the war was justified. We were in trouble. But did I want to be involved? No. So they assigned me the job of essentially diagnosing mentally challenged soldiers at the general hospital in Chicago. Just a lucky break, I guess. I was able to go home every night.

One of the things that made a huge impression on me was, in World War I, you were punished if you tried to get out. And punished severely. You would get a dishonorable discharge and maybe time in the brig.[1] People would go so far as to wet their bed to get discharged. In World War II, if you did the same thing, the attitude was totally different. The authorities felt that anyone who wanted to get out of the war that badly must be sick in the head. So people like that received a medical discharge.

The other thing that impressed me was the administrative practicality of some of the things we did. If a guy came into the psychiatric unit, and he was a hero—won lots of medals in the war and stuff like that—and then suddenly had gone AWOL, the practice was to give him a medical discharge and let him out.[2] If he was not a hero, and just a troublemaker, they would give him a discharge without honor. But the same qualities that make you a hero often make you a troublemaker. And it was interesting that the very same behavior could elicit entirely different results.

There were all kinds of soldiers, but there were basically two different kinds of people, and you could diagnose this part instantly. If they were neurotic, you'd ask them what was wrong, and they'd sit there and talk for an hour and a half, telling you all their problems. If they were nuts—psychotic—they'd say nothing. They would say, "What's wrong with *you*? Nothing's wrong with *me*."

They had to open up because they had no choice. I remember one guy who was brought in by MPs.[3] I asked, "Well, how'd you get here?" And he said, "They brought me down to headquarters in Chicago and transferred me here." I said, "Why?" He said, "There's no reason, I don't know why." And so I said: "Tell me the story." Turned out he'd been in North Carolina on furlough.[4] When he returned by train to Chicago, he said, "At the train station, I heard them saying over the loudspeaker that they were looking for an undertaker because they were about to kill me." And he said, "I got so scared, I ran over to one of the MPs and told him, 'Please protect me, they're going to kill me!'" Instead of protecting him, they sent him to our hospital for treatment. And he couldn't figure out why.

Private First Class, U.S. Army

We usually used electroshock therapy, which was a spectacular treatment. Very effective. It's still used today. We also had a room where fifty or sixty patients waited to be given insulin to put them into shock instead of the electricity. The room was three-quarters dark, with nurses running around holding orange juice and syringes loaded with sugar. As the patients became unconscious, some would start shaking all over. If the nurses got to them in time, they'd give them orange juice orally. But if they didn't, they had to give them an injection of sugar to pull them out.

I had a peculiar experience once. My dad was a doctor, and he had a couple of drugstores in the area. I loved to work in them, fool around, and sell things. I usually stopped by on my way home from the hospital. I never bothered to change out of my uniform and into civilian clothes. One day, a bunch of MPs came in to arrest me for being AWOL. I said, "I'm not AWOL!" They were skeptical: "Well, you're here every single day." They finally checked it out, but for a minute they were convinced I was trying to get out of my duties.

---

1 *Brig* is a colloquial term for a U.S. military jail, typically used by Navy and Marine personnel.

2 *AWOL* is a military term for desertion, an acronym for "absent without leave."

3 *MP* is an acronym for members of the Military Police Corps, the U.S. Army's law-enforcement branch.

4 *Furlough* is a military term for an approved leave of absence from duty.

Mary COBB

I COULD HARDLY WAIT TO GRADUATE from high school and join the military. I wanted to join the Navy, but I had bad eyesight. If I had to evacuate a ship and couldn't find my glasses, I'd be in a hell of a mess! I wanted to be a lab technician when I was younger, because I was interested in that phase of medicine. But I could not afford to go to college. I got into nurses training in my hometown of Reading, Pennsylvania, without any problem. I did that for three years before being sent to the 131st General Hospital in Blandford, England.

We weren't too far from the train depot, and we were also near Royal Air Force field. They could fly the patients in and then transport them from the plane to our base via the little old Army ambulances. The injured came in roughly once a week, maybe more often at first. They had received first aid treatment on the battlefield. When they were well enough, they were sent to a hospital like ours—which they called "spiders." The building had one central area where all the charting was done, all the sterilizing of instruments and that kind of stuff. The wards branched off the center—three wards to the south and three wards to the north. It was kind of like a spider. And that's why they called them that.

I mainly worked in orthopedics, so I saw all kinds of fractures or broken bones, from shoulders to arms to legs to what have you. Treating orthopedics then and treating orthopedics today is very, very different. I kind of have to laugh when I think about that, how they treated patients with broken bones and stuff. If they had a fractured leg or, say, a femur, they got a pin put through the bone, the beginning of the bone. They got a pin in there, and then they'd hook it onto a pulley with a weight so that the weight would help to pull the bone back into shape.

It was hard to keep a straight face while dealing with patients. We had a British lieutenant who was so severely injured, shot up in every part of his body. He just had so many things wrongs. Burns, fractures—I really don't know how he survived. He's one patient I will never forget. Sometimes it used to help to kid around, which I was pretty good at. I liked to kid the patients. I know that kind of thing works for me too when I'm feeling a little down in the dumps and somebody says something funny, or "C'mon Mary, it isn't all that bad." That's how I handled it.

One day a patient said, "Lieutenant! Do you mind if I call you Sparky?" Patients weren't supposed to call us by nicknames, they were supposed to call us lieutenant. All nurses at that time were lieutenants, second or first, except a charge nurse, which usually was an older person with more education and qualified to be a captain.[1] I didn't care about that and said, "You do as you want to do." "Well," he said, "I'm going to call you Sparky because your eyes sparkle." So that was that. That was my nickname, especially on that ward. They were doing something that they weren't supposed to do, and they liked that.

I was always happy when I saw them being picked up in an ambulance and transported to a ship going home. It was always a wonderful thing to see that, as bad as they were when they came into our hospital, they were healed enough to make the trip back home and to continue their treatment at hospitals in the States. That was the highlight of my job as a nurse—to see them go home.

---

1 A charge nurse is the supervisor of the ward, overseeing the care of patients and assigning duties to the nurses on staff.

2 The U.S. Army Nurse Corps dates back to the Revolutionary War, and is the oldest women's military organization. Although numbering less than seven thousand before World War II, nearly sixty thousand nurses joined and served in the Army Nurse Corps during the war. Nurses served in all environments, from the front lines to transport ships and planes to field hospitals and at home.

First Lieutenant, U.S. Army Nurse Corps[2]

LIFE MEMBER
VFW
2323

"I spent five years in the Army.
I was a damn good soldier."

Opposite: **John AIMONETTI, Private First Class, U.S. Army**
Preceding spread: **Bernard SADOWSKI, Corporal, U.S. Marines; Joseph MANKOWSKI, Lieutenant Second Grade, U.S. Navy**

Morton GOLLIN

Second Lieutenant, U.S. Army Air Corps

WE WERE ASSIGNED TO BOMB THE Blechhammer oil refineries in Slawiecice, Poland, but were bombarded with flak over the target and started limping back home out of formation.[1] We were dropped to ten thousand feet in altitude from our original twenty-one. The gunners were complaining bitterly about getting soaked with gasoline, which was leaking in the waist of the plane. Any one bullet would have blown us sky high, so we decided to abandon ship. As navigator, I gave them instructions, told them what the altitude was, and everybody said goodbye. I was in the nose of the plane with the gunner. We were surprised to see the door open so beautifully. We shook hands, and I dropped down to find myself half in, half out of the plane—my parachute harness had caught on the door and I was swinging in the breeze! Now, if I had been a real officer instead of a civilian in my head, I wouldn't be here today, because protocol says that I should have let the enlisted gunner go out first. Just like the captain is the last one to leave the ship.

The second I got unhooked into the air, it was a wonderful feeling. You get more of a drop in an elevator than you do leaving a plane. A plane is going forward at about two hundred miles per hour, so when you drop, your body is also going forward at two hundred miles per hour, slowing down into an arc on a parabola. I was just sitting on my cushion of air looking around, glorying in the moment, and I completely forget that we were at ten thousand feet. I thought we were still at twenty, so I delayed my count, not wanting to freeze my butt off until I got down. I saw the ground rushing up at me, and I desperately pulled my chute. I landed in a field of grain that felt like a featherbed, but the fact that I delayed so long meant that I hit the ground about a quarter mile away from the others. Their chutes had opened right away, and they floated to a place where they were met by German soldiers and captured immediately.

I buried my parachute under a haystack and started walking. I looked up and saw a little creek wrapping around a little hill. Looking like they were sitting on bleachers, a group of people on the hill were watching me. Two men came toward me and established that they were Czechs. They offered to help me and took me to a thicket of trees. I laid down there, and they made me understand that they would be back for me about midnight.

After sitting there for hours, I felt restless. I'm too impatient a person, so I decided to start walking. I got to a little village, scared some children who were playing in the streets, and met some people who took me into a house and gave me some beer—it wasn't very good. I tried to give them some money—everybody gets an escape kit when they go on a mission, it had maps, our hard chocolate D-bar, and fifty American dollars. I tried to give the money to the people who were helping me, but they said they'd be killed by the Germans if they were found with American money on them. A man took me to a little concrete bunker to hide and indicated he'd be back at midnight. I thought, "Here we go again," but I waited. When he returned, he gave me some clothes—corduroys and a jacket that I pulled over my khakis—and advised me to walk in a southwesterly direction, where I ought to be able to find some Yugoslav partisans to help me out.

The Russian lines were one hundred and fifty miles to the east. Italy was twelve hundred miles to the southwest. I decided to join the Russians. Big, big mistake. If I had been caught several days further in toward the Russian lines, I probably would have been shot. I arrived at a bridge with a lot of foot traffic and bikes going across. There was nobody at the sentry post, so I started to cross. I got halfway when the sentry comes around the corner. Well, it was impossible to turn around and go backward, so I went past him, gave him a Heil Hitler, and kept going until I heard, "Halt!" I turned around and he had his rifle up.

I stopped and tried to explain to him in gibberish that I was a Romanian worker. I kept saying, "*Nicht verstehe, nicht verstehe* ("I don't understand.")." He patted me down, didn't find anything, and the two of us sat in the little sentry house waiting for somebody he'd called to arrive. For some reason he decided to pat me down again, and in doing so, he found the stuff in the khakis underneath my new clothes—maps and things. He pulled out his Luger, scaring me to death. I was twenty years old; he was in his sixties. He was more scared than me. I could see his hand shaking, and I was afraid he was going to shoot me accidentally. Then a well-dressed gentleman arrived—Gestapo, undoubtedly—and conferred with the old guard.[2] He told me in faultless English, "I'm sorry, we made a mistake. You can go on your way." I looked at him, and he's waiting for me to scoot away so he can grab me. I said, "*Nicht verstehe.*"

After two weeks in a civilian prison, they transferred me around until I made it to the main Gestapo headquarters. I was not cooperative during the interrogations. I gave them name, rank, serial number. Somehow you're indoctrinated to reveal nothing. You don't think of yourself as doing it patriotically; you're doing it because you have a sense of duty. They put me into handcuffs and shoved me into a cell with no bed. By my third day, I had figured out the German mentality: you had to scream loud. You had to scream louder than they did. So I started yelling, "Commandant. I want the commandant!" I kept on yelling and wouldn't shut up until they got an officer. I told him, "I'm an American, I want to be in a prison camp, Geneva regulations."

The next day, they took me out of that place and I was put on a train in the company of five Americans whose plane had been shot down the day before. We were headed to the main interrogation center, Dulag Luft.[3] At the train station, I told the guard I had to go to the bathroom, and he said, "Go." I said, "Aren't you afraid I'm going to try to escape?" He looked me in the eyes and said, "Go. Try to escape. You're dead if you do. A civilian will kill you. I have to protect you." And he was telling the truth. Frankfurt had been bombed so heavily that people would kill any American they found out of rage.

At Dulag Luft, it was the same game as all the other interrogation places. The seemingly friendly interrogator offered me a cigarette and said, "Here, just fill this out and then we can send you to a very nice prison camp. The war will be over for you." I put down my name, rank, serial number, and he told me to fill in the rest. I said, "That's all you get." And he in turn: "You're going to regret this. I can send you back to the Gestapo and they won't be so easy on you this time." Six hours later, I got called back in front of this interrogator. He told me, "I wish I could keep you, but we're so damn crowded, I can't. But let me just show you something." He put the paper in front of me. Everything is filled out. They knew my grandmother's middle name. They knew the day I graduated gunnery school. They knew everything.

We're an open society. When a guy graduates gunnery school or navigation school, it's printed in the *Milwaukee Journal Sentinel*. The Nazis had a system for compiling information. They had real drive. When I was sixteen years old in Milwaukee, which was a heavily German town, a friend of mine and I would climb on the roof of a garage and watch the Nazi *Bund* meetings in the yard next door.[4] They were marching around, saluting. Until the war started, Hitler was a hero to the Germans, even American Germans. And I'm Jewish, so it was especially scary to watch. Hitlerites existed everywhere in the States. We imprisoned all of the Japanese who were probably good American citizens, but we never touched the Germans.

I was put in Stalag Luft III, which was southeast of Berlin.[5] That was the real beginning of being a prisoner of war. The soldier questioning me made me fill out a form, and when it came to religion, I hesitated. He looked up and said, "Ah, it's okay in here. You don't have to worry about that." Then he put down "H" for Hebrew. He was telling me in essence that the Luftwaffe camps were not treating Jews any differently than the rest, and I found that to be true. I had no problems. The Luftwaffe held to the Geneva regulations as best they could.

We were in the camp until about the 28th of January, in the coldest winter Germany had seen for many, many years. That day we could hear the Russian's guns going off ten miles away. The Germans decided to march us out of the camp. They permitted us to break into a barracks and take whatever we wanted. I made the terrible mistake of taking a new pair of shoes that were a fraction too big. During the five-day walk in the cold and snow, those new shoes cut into me, creating a deep, bleeding "V." With the frostbite, that march was the most painful part of my prisoner experience. As we marched, they burned the camp down behind us. Eventually they stuffed us in boxcars for a few days, until we were dropped off at camp Stalag VIIA outside of Moosburg, near Munich. There must have been two hundred thousand people there. Russians, Americans, and people from all over Europe. There was no food. Some of the people had been in the camp for years. It was a really bad time.

I was in that camp from February 7th to April 29th, when Patton's Third Army liberated us. There are two things I remember from that day. The soldiers gave us white bread. We had not seen bread that had anything in it other than sawdust for a long time. That was the best cake we had ever eaten! And I remember two friends of mine and I jumped the fence, walked across fields until we came to a house. There was a German man, woman, and daughter in that house—scared to death. "We don't want to harm you," I told them. "There is only one thing we do want, if you'll give it to us: draw a bath. Each one of us is going to take a bath, one at a time."

For sixty years, I never talked about being a prisoner of war. It wasn't until I saw a panel on someone's truck in Palm Springs with the name "General Patton" inscribed on it. I don't know why, but out of the blue I asked this stranger, "Where were you on April 29th, 1945?" He looked up at me and he says, "I was liberating a prisoner-of-war camp in Moosburg, Germany." I put out my hand and I said, "Thank you very, very much." He introduced me to another local guy, Tom Gibbons, who was also in the Third Army and liberated my camp. Now he's my best buddy.

---

1 Blechhammer was an area in Nazi Germany that contained prisoner-of-war camps as well as refineries that converted coal into synthetic oil. These plants were a strategic target for American bombers.

2 The Gestapo was the secret, political police force of Nazi Germany. They were charged with identifying and incarcerating anyone considered to be a threat to the Nazi party, and operated with few restrictions.

3 A contraction of *Durchgangslager*, or "entrance camp," Dulag Luft was the name given to transit camps intended specifically for Air Force personnel, and were used primarily for the interrogation of captured pilots and aircrew before transport to other prisoner-of-war camps.

4 An organization of ethnic Germans living in America, the German American *Bund* was established in the 1930s and promoted Nazi ideology and anti-Semitism.

5 Stalag Luft was the name for prisoner-of-war camps intended specifically for captured Allied aircrew. Stalag Luft III was located in Zagan, Poland, approximately one hundred miles southeast of Berlin.

POW ★ MI

I LANDED IN MARSEILLES ON AUGUST 25th, 1944, and worked with the Seventh Army under General Patch, moving north through France as the Third Army moved toward the east. Fortunately, my division was moved to the Third Army and joined forces with my idol, George Patton.[1] The closer you were to the front during combat, the more you adored the man. The further you were in rear echelon, the more you despised him. The men in the back couldn't stand him, because he wore their buns off getting us food, ammunition, and fuel. When I hear anybody from the Third Army badmouth Patton, I already know where they were in the scheme of things.

I was with a mechanized reconnaissance squadron. It was the horse cavalry reconstituted. We were highly armored, highly fast, highly mobile. So it was our function to precede the rest of the troops. We were the first ones to find out where the German strength was, and if we couldn't handle it, we'd back off and wait for the big boys to come behind us. The difference between General Patch and Patton was that if we went out on recon for Patch and got in trouble, his *modus operandi* was: "Okay, get the hell back." Patton would go get us. He moved heaven and earth. Who would you rather work for?

The Battle of Metz was very quick and swift but high-casualty.[2] Some reporters were on Patton's back because of the casualty rate. He responded, "Would you rather that it took me three days and I lost ten thousand a day?" That was his attitude. Hit them hard and hit them fast and hit them with everything you got. During the Battle of the Bulge, a very bright German general named von Rundstedt decided that he was going to break through our lines and head directly toward Antwerp where ninety percent of our supplies were dumped. If he broke through in Antwerp, he'd cut off our supply lines and divide the English, Canadian, Australian, and some American troops from the rest of us. Eisenhower asked his generals who could head him off and when. There wasn't a general that could do it in less than ten days. A famous British general said it would take at least two weeks. But Patton said, "Three days." And we were there in three days. That was Patton. If you're in war, you better be in there to win and not to pussyfoot around, or they're going to beat the hell out of you.

I loved outfits like the 101st Airborne. The 3rd Infantry Division, the 36th Division, and the 45th Division were all really top notch—and I did reconnaissance for all of them. Once my unit was committed to action, we stayed in action. It's not like we fought for a week and took leave for a week. I had one hundred and eighty-seven days of straight combat, and one day of euphoria. And that day was on April 29th, 1945, when I broke through the gate of a POW camp and freed eleven thousand guys.

That was Stalag VIIA.[3] We had a twenty-four-hour notice that the deranged bastard, Hitler, had ordered the execution of eleven thousand American POWs held there. Stalag VIIA had about one hundred and thirty thousand POWs total. Russia, the Ukraine, Greece, Turkey, England, Australia, France, Germany—there were thirty-some-odd nations represented there. We had a little less than a day to put together what's known as a combat

Colonel Corporal, U.S. Army

command team. Hitler had ordered a detachment of six hundred black-shirt SS, real scum of the Earth, to handle the execution.[4] We were fifty kilometers away. We had to travel all night, most of it behind the German lines, to get to that camp before the SS did. We caught them a mile and a half from the camp. They never got closer than a half a mile to the gate. Not one POW was hurt.

My tank was the first one in to the compound. We were surrounded in less than two heartbeats by three hundred and sixty degrees of vast humanity. I had to yell down to cut the engines because I was afraid of the prisoners getting under the treads of the tank. Some of them had been there for many years; some of the Brits had been there since El Alamein in Africa. Some of them had been in Dunkirk when they retreated from France back to England. Some of the Russians had been there the longest. When we put the American flag up, their cheer could be heard back at the Statue of Liberty.

I was involved in the liberation of Buchenwald and a satellite camp some miles away.[5] The people were skeletons, thinner than a hanger you would hang a dress on, all in a pajama kind of garb, and the stench was unbelievable. They were so skeletal, I couldn't determine their age or sex. Some of them were like automatons walking toward you, their arms outstretched. They would hug you and not let go. They realized what was happening, that they were free. We immediately gave them all our food—and that was the worst thing we could have done. Their digestive tracks could not stand some of the food, and some of them died as a consequence. We should have just waited for the people coming up behind us to assess. Many of us were nineteen-, twenty-year-old kids. We didn't know.

Now I am an honorary member of the Jewish War Veterans, where I am known as the "Righteous Gentile." I suppose every part of the country has groups of speakers, because they don't want the Holocaust to fade out of history. Very often a group of us speaks at high-school assemblies, and I always tell the kids that when I was seventeen, I was sitting exactly where they're sitting now, and at nineteen, I was witnessing the reality of the Holocaust. There are idiots out there trying to disclaim the fact that the Holocaust happened.

When I returned to the States right after the war, I decided to meet with some of the families of soldiers who had died. The first one was in Indianapolis in a working-class neighborhood with row homes. There was no furniture in the living room, they had set up a chair semicircle, with one facing the rows of chairs. Every aunt, uncle, cousin, brother, sister, the father, the mother, the grandparents were all there. I was twenty at that point. How do you explain to a family the death of their son? The fact is I had spoken with him five minutes before he was killed. He was decapitated so I didn't tell them how he died—except that he died instantly with no pain, and what a great guy he was. The conversation turned around and—it's completely understandable—they asked how come I survived. Survivor's guilt, I later found out, is extremely oppressive. I cancelled all the other appointments because that one was sufficient. The most important thing to remember about this was: the true heroes are the ones who never came home. They're the ones. When I do eulogies for veterans, I key off Matthew 5—"Blessed are the peacemakers, for they shall be called the children of God."

---

1 General George S. Patton commanded the U.S. Third Army as it advanced across France in late 1944 and 1945, and was known for his rapid deployment of armored forces in frontal assaults.

2 The Battle of Metz occurred from September to December 1944, between German and U.S. forces, in and around the French city of Metz. Both sides suffered heavy casualties before the U.S. Third Army secured the city.

3 Located in the town of Moosburg, in Bavaria, Germany, Stalag VIIA was the largest prisoner-of-war camp in Germany. After defeating the defending German troops, the camp was liberated by the Fourteenth Armored Division on April 29th, 1945. Due to this and the liberation of other camps, the division earned the nickname "the Liberators."

4 The Schutzstaffel (SS), or "protective squadron," was a Nazi paramilitary organization that was fiercely loyal to Hitler and the Nazi ideology. Under the command of Nazi party leader and military commander Heinrich Himmler, the SS were responsible for numerous war crimes, including much of the organizing and implementation of the Holocaust.

5 Buchenwald was a concentration camp located near Weimar, Germany. Unlike a prisoner-of-war camp, the majority held there were religious and political prisoners from all over Europe and Russia. Constructed in 1937, it is estimated more than fifty thousand prisoners died at Buchenwald before its liberation by Allied forces in 1945.

"When a young German POW asked me what freedom felt like, I just took it for granted because I was born and raised as a Jewish American."

Opposite: **Mordecai "Morty" RESNICK, Dental Technician, U.S. Army**
Following spread: **Bill FINKLE, Captain, U.S. Army; Aldo BRUNO, Seabee Second Class, U.S. Navy**

חי

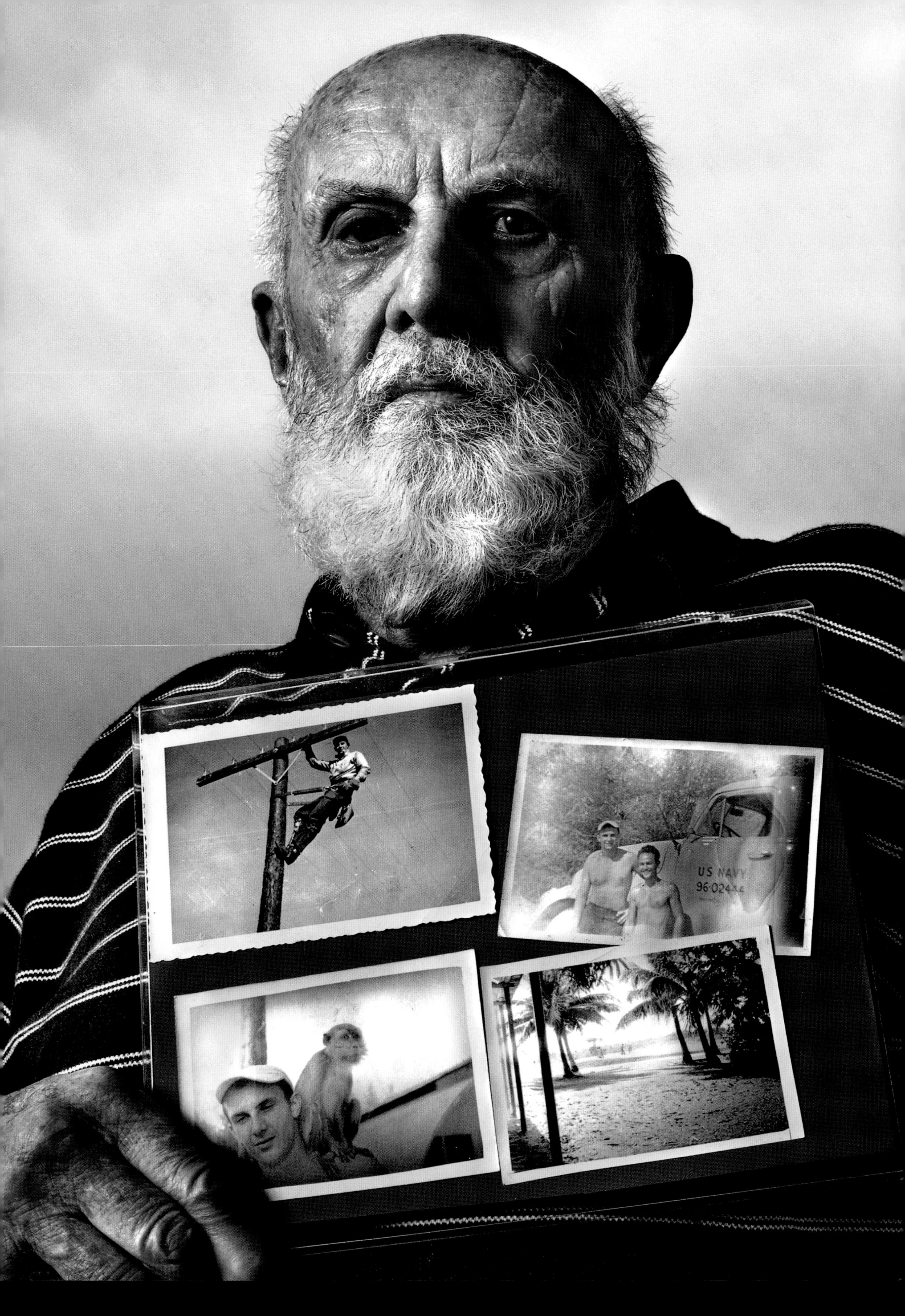
US NAVY
96-02444

Ed ROYCE

AFTER GETTING TURNED DOWN BY the Navy for bad eyesight, believe it or not, the Army put me in an observation battalion. My outfit went to France in the middle of July 1944. We were with Patton's Third Army, and he liked to keep things moving. We were the forward observers, and stayed ahead of everyone else, reporting back on troop movement and advising the best strategies for attack.

We kept an eye out for enemy targets, like tanks, infantry, or whatever else they were bringing to bear. One of the main targets was artillery. We'd triangulate on the muzzle flash, which is the flare of light caused by gunpowder igniting. It would help us pick up targets at night. If we were able to get two or more observation posts to see the same target, we could triangulate the position of the enemy attack. We'd relay the info and our guys would take care of it. But the Germans were pretty crafty. They would use flashless powder on their tanks or move their guns, so they were very hard to spot.

Of course, the Germans were trying to pick us up, too. They had their observers looking for our observers. One time we had a post in a forestry tower—it was the tallest darn thing. It was like an oil derrick, we were way up there. The Germans put charges at the bottom and blew off all four corners. The tower had cross-braces that fortunately held the thing up. That night, the wind was blowing and that tower would creak and groan and sway, and we would think, "Oh, it's going over!" Then it would hang there for a little while and sway back. That was one of the scariest nights, but we were lucky.

On April 29th, the 45th and 42nd Divisions liberated Dachau.[1] One of our lieutenants told us we could go take a look if we wanted to. We jumped in a jeep and drove over, and we were absolutely astonished by what we found. It had only been liberated for a few hours. The prisoners were skin and bones, but they were happy as the dickens to see us. They were either happy to see us, or they were determined to kill the German guards. Some of our troops were, too. I saw one guard running away from this big crowd of prisoners, and somebody shot him in the face. He staggered around and leaned up against a tree, and the prisoners caught up with him and just beat him to death. It sounds kind of inhumane, but if you had seen what they had done to their prisoners, it was far from surprising.

I found an office with beautiful little statues, about a foot and a half high, of different military figures. One was of an SS officer on a horse, holding the Nazi flag; another one was Barbarossa on a horse, carrying a banner.[2] I was picking them up and studying the craftsmanship when a bunch of the prisoners came crashing through the door and smashed all these statues in fury.

I took pictures during the war, and my last eight were of Dachau. Pictures of a train with bodies in the cars, stacks of clothing before the people went into the gas chamber, and the people piled chest-high inside.

When the war ended, I set up a photo lab in the beautiful town of Salzburg. A lot of other guys had taken pictures, and I developed their film, too. Once in a while I'd see something that was worth saving and would make a print for myself. One guy who had been in Italy had pictures of when they caught Mussolini.[3] And so I made copies of his photos of Mussolini after the partisans had caught him and had hanged him and his girlfriend Petacci upside-down.

It was an interesting process, watching all these collected images of the war—the hell we'd been through, the triumph, the devastation, liberation—come to the surface. To just stand there and look at the photos and say, "That's a good one."

---

1 Located near the town of Dachau, Germany, the Dachau concentration camp was established in 1933 by the Nazi government. The first of its kind, the camp initially held political prisoners, but by the time of its liberation in 1945, it held over sixty thousand prisoners of various types, including more than twenty thousand Jews.

2 Frederick I, nicknamed Barbarossa for his red beard, was a popular monarch of medieval Germany. Elected king of Germany in 1152, and crowned Holy Roman Emporer in 1155, he died in 1190 while marching with his army during the Third Crusade.

3 Benito Mussolini was a leader of the National Fascist Party in Italy, and prime minister of the country from 1922 to 1943. Under Mussolini, Italy sided with the Axis powers in World War II and declared war on Britain and France in 1940, and Russia and the United States in 1941. In 1943, he was ousted by members of the Fascist government, and while attempting to flee the country with mistress his Clara Petacci, he was caught and killed by Italian resistance fighters in 1945.

Private First Class, U.S. Army

Opposite: **John Senter, Seaman, U.S. Coast Guard** Above: **Frank PIETROCARLI, Aviation Ordnanceman Second Class, U.S. Navy**

I COMPLETED SIXTY-SEVEN COMBAT missions in my P-51 Mustang.[1] On my sixty-eighth, I was shot down. I was in northern Germany strafing locomotives when we ran into one hundred and fifty German fighters. There were planes being shot down all over the place, and my airplane hit high-tension wires. It damaged the airplane so badly, the left gun came right out through the spar and the inboard gun came up at a thirty-degree angle through the wing. All the ammo panels on top of the wing tore off and took the horizontal stabilizer with them. The only way I could keep the plane in the air was with a lot of power, but an oil leak caused the engine to quit. I was able to keep the plane airborne long enough to try to bail out, but when I let the canopy go, I realized I was too low. The treetops were whistling by and I decided to belly it into the trees, but just as the plane started to stall out, a nice long field opened up right in front of me and I slid right up in between two German houses.

By the time I got out, a farmer was yelling and coming at me with a pitchfork. I threw my parachute in his direction and ran into the woods. I had an escape-and-evasion packet with me that had a map, but I couldn't recognize any of the names. This was in the middle of January, and it was the coldest winter on record in Europe. If you stayed still for fifteen minutes, you would freeze. So I started walking west. I knew I was in northern Germany, and figured if I could get into Holland, maybe I could get into friendly territory.

I was twenty-one years old, and surprisingly wasn't scared. I was only ten years removed from playing hide-and-seek, except now I was playing it with the Germans. At night I'd walk on the roads and in daytime I'd walk in the fields and through the trees. There was nothing to eat other than a few sugar tablets from my escape kit. I tried to dig a turnip out of the frozen field and broke my knife. When I walked, my feet would sweat. When I stopped walking, they froze. The hair on my head was frozen and breaking off. I must have been a pretty sight.

At four in the morning of the second night, I came to a bridge guarded by a soldier who was stamping his feet and blowing on his hands. If I had turned around I would have looked suspicious, so I just kept going. As I got up to him, I blew on my hands and muttered some gibberish because I certainly didn't know any German! And he was blowing on his hands, and said something back to me which I couldn't understand. I kept on going, waiting for a bullet or a challenge or something. I finally went got over the hill and out of his sight. I turned around to see what he was doing—he was still standing there, stamping his feet, blowing on his hands, trying to keep warm.

I came across a group of children ice skating on wooden shoes, clogs that turned up at the ends. I thought, "Well, maybe I'm in Holland!" The children looked at me and pointed, and one of them ran up to a little white house. That's when I thought, "I'm not in Holland." So I took off through the trees. About a minute later I heard a voice yelling "Halt! Halt!" I heard two shots, and the bullets crossed over my head through the twigs and the trees. So I stood there with my hands up; at this point I didn't control my own life. And the thoughts you have at gray, unusual times! As that man was coming up to me, my mind said, "I sure hope that man's wife was good to him last night." He took me back to this little white house, and it was full of people and they fed me. They gave me a cup of tea and fed me two pieces of black bread with margarine and jam, which is the first food I'd had since I had taken off three days before. That's how I was captured.

I was taken to a German Luftwaffe base.[2] The Germans were flying in and out, and it was frustrating. Here I was, an American fighter pilot, and all these guys were flying around and I couldn't shoot them down. But they didn't treat me badly at all. They did take my pneumatic G-suit, as they'd never seen one before.[3] There wasn't a jail, so I stayed in the guardhouse. When the guards were off duty, they ate and slept there. After a couple of days I got to know them, particularly one guard who would bring in a German paper and teach me German. He had been a prisoner of war in Wisconsin in World War I, and I helped him refresh his English. We had a great time.

They took me to an interrogation camp in Oberursel, where they took lots of pilots.[4] They had found my airplane, naturally, and had taken film of the locomotives we destroyed that I had shot for documentation. I wouldn't acknowledge that it was my airplane. They showed me a book that they had of my fighter group: who was there, who the commanders were, who was shot down. They knew more about me than I did. I was put into solitary confinement for nine days.

Finally I admitted to it. They already had all the information. In the middle of February we ended up in Nuremberg, which was in very bad decay. I was put in a group of six other pilots. When Patton crossed the Rhine, we were on a death march to a camp in Moosberg, near Munich. We didn't walk in the daytime. There wasn't that much security, mainly because our guards were very old. They were probably fifty and sixty years old. It was not unusual after ten days to see an American on one side of a guard carrying a briefcase and his knapsack, and another on the other side, carrying his gun. We did not want to lose our Luftwaffe guards, because with regular German Army guards, we would have had it very tough.

The day we were liberated, we could hear the guns coming for quite a while. The night before, the German guards all lined up, marched out the gate, and left. When the Americans arrived, there was a battle that lasted about an hour outside the gates. We were all in slip trenches, the bullets were whizzing by—and then our tanks came rolling in. At that point we could say we lived through the war.

I was put on huge troop ship, but there were only about three hundred and fifty of us on it—of which one hundred and twenty were French nurses. I think that's where bikinis started, because they would roll down their brassieres and roll up their panties into little strips. We all laid out on the sun decks and enjoyed the trip home immensely.

---

1 Designed by the North American Aviation Company and debuting in 1940, the P-51 Mustang was a fast, long-range fighter plane that played a critical role in escorting Allied bombers.

2 The Luftwaffe was the air force of the German military during World War II. Officially founded in 1935, but having existed in various forms since World War I, the Luftwaffe was one of the most powerful air forces in the world at the start of the war.

3 A G-suit is worn by aviators to protect their bodies from the effects of acceleration. A series of pressurized bladders prevents blood draining from the brain by applying force to the abdomen and legs, thereby preventing loss of consciousness for pilots contending with extended periods of acceleration.

4 Oberursel is a German town, northwest of Frankfurt, that served as a transport hub and interrogation center, operated by the Luftwaffe, primarily for captured Allied airmen before they were sent to a permanent POW camp.

Colonel, U.S. Air Force

Above: **Tom FISHER, Pilot, U.S. Army Air Corps** Opposite: **George GAMPER, Private First Class, U.S. Air Force**

THE LST—LANDING SHIP TANK—was designed to go up on sandy beaches.[1] It had the big bow doors, and a ramp would come down so that trucks, jeeps, and tanks could drive directly onto the beach. It was bare bones metal and very light. It couldn't be very deep in the water to land on the beach. It didn't go more than eight feet deep. When it was traveling through big waves, the front and rear ends would go up and you could see the ship bellied in the middle. You could actually see that ship bend.

We had heard of Okinawa, but we had no idea that it was going to be one of the fiercest battles at the close of the war.[2] We became a fleet post office: we were anchored in a bay at Okinawa, and all the ships would send a small boat over to pick up the mail, which was dropped by aircraft on our deck. We were sitting ducks in that bay, and the kamikazes were abundant. An LST four hundred feet away from us got hit, and that made us a little jumpy.

James Mueller in uniform.

Once those kamikaze guys got in the neighborhood, a lot of them didn't get through. Twenty ships would be firing on the same plane. I was positioned on a 40mm gun. Believe me, the adrenaline was going when you were turning that wheel and trying to shoot them down. All you were worried about was getting that plane out of the air before it came down on you. Sometimes these Marine pilots would catch up with them as they were coming over, and our shelling would hit them. When we realized we hit a Marine plane, all we could do was shrug our shoulders; it just happened. They were chasing Japanese planes and we were throwing lead. Shells going here and there and up that way. We never knew for sure if we did it, or if it was the ship next to us. It was what they called "friendly fire." Not very friendly.

Machinist, U.S. Navy

We were in that mode for about four months, and then when the first atomic bomb was dropped, Operation Post Office ceased. After the second bomb, we prepared to head to Japan, and on our way a typhoon happened. We were advised by the fleet admiral to seek shelter at a little resort area called Wakayama. They had a nice big bay there, but they didn't have high enough mountains, and the winds just pushed us. We dropped our bow anchor and our stern anchor and put the engines in reverse, but we still got blown into the sea wall that was protecting this little town. And we rested there for a month until the fleet tugboat could come and pull us off the reef.

Really funny thing about it was that the villagers there knew the war was over, and here's this big ship stuck to their island. So the people, curious, came down to the sea wall. And, lo and behold, they start singing "Coming Around the Mountain" in English: "She'll be coming around the mountain..." We started singing back to them. They asked us for cigarettes and chewing gum. Anytime we saw them, we waved and said, "Heyyy!" and they smiled back.

---

1 The Landing Ship Tank was developed by the military as an ocean-going ship able to deliver armored infantry and vehicles to shore during amphibious operations.

2 The Battle of Okinawa was the last major battle of the Pacific War. The largest Allied amphibious assault, it stretched from April to June 1945, with the objective of securing a base of operations within striking distance of mainland Japan. It resulted in one of the highest casualty rates of any World War II conflict, with more than one hundred thousand Japanese and fifty thousand Allied casualties, as well as more than one hundred thousand civilian casualties.

US

Sergeant, U.S. Army

Licata and fellow soldiers during basic training at Camp Roberts in central California.

we invaded the Philippines and Okinawa. We were losing one medic a week—either killed or seriously wounded. I saw things that caused me to wake up sweating and shaking for many years. Like hearing young sailors crying for their mothers in the middle of the night. Or telling men they were going to be all right when I knew they were going to die.

As a medic, I saw a great deal of blood and suffering. The most haunting memory: I found a man with his face slashed off—flopped over like a Halloween mask. I thought he was dead. So I went over to pick him up, and the minute my hand touched the body, he said, "Ow! You're hurting me!" That got me.

Despite these experiences, I was lucky. I could feel the power of my mother's prayers. Felt to me like I was just lifted up, floating on air. I could hear her voice, too. Like the first and only time they issued us hamburgers. I was in charge of a group of medics, and before we started to eat, I told the boys, "Let's go wash our hands first." I was hearing my mother then. Meanwhile, the enemies got a direct hit right where we had been sitting. When we came back, the hamburgers had all been knocked to pieces.

During the invasion of Okinawa, I was walking along the front when I picked up a Japanese bugle and randomly tooted the song they play when the horse race takes off on at the racetrack: da-da-da-dun-dun-dun-dun-dun-dun-dun. I had been a trumpet player in the high-school band, and thought it would lighten up the mood. Right after I put the bugle down, eight Japanese soldiers came out of a cave with their hands up in the air. They thought it was an attack, so they came out to surrender! That story made it to the paper back in my hometown of Los Gatos. The headline referred to me as "The Pied Piper of Okinawa."

I had a lot of close calls. When I witnessed Japanese cannon fire pin an American soldier under a tree, I dived into the line of fire to pull him out. Everyone stared at me with dropped jaws when we walked away from the shelling. My commanding officer grabbed me and yelled, "You certainly deserve a medal, and I'm going to see that you get one!" Then he told me to pull down my pants because I got shot. "No, I'm fine," I told him. But he made me look. By god, sure enough, I was hit right between the legs! Several minutes later he was killed. As a medic, it was one of my duties to issue Purple Hearts, and I thought it was fair to give myself a Purple Heart that day.

"A lot of good guys never came home. My mom walked to the neighborhood church to pray for me every day. I was one of the lucky ones."

Joe NICASSIO, Seaman First Class, U.S. Navy

U.S. NAVY

Louis (right) with brother Frank Lezon.

Louis LEZON

In late December 1942, I was assigned to a Carrier Aircraft Service Unit in Fort Island, Hawaii. On the way to my outfit, our ship passed the remains of the Japanese attack: planes and ships underwater, the water filled with oil. We were called to stand at attention and hand-salute because the divers were bringing up a black bag from the oily waters. We didn't know what it was, but we stood and saluted. I was just a young lad; it was touching.

At Kaneohe Bay, I serviced planes that were coming in from the mainland. This usually consisted of draining the antifreeze to prepare them for the warmer weather down south. Once my crew and I were assigned to replace a gas tank, and it wasn't aligning properly. An impatient officer among the others asked, "Can I get my foot in there yet?" I looked up to find a gentleman in a flight suit that said Commander O'Hare. He was a big lanky guy. He stuck his long leg in there and took a couple of pokes and said, "I'm satisfied. Get it all together, let me know what the outcome is. I'm missing out on my flights." After it was assembled, to my dismay, I was told that it was no good. One of the chiefs said, "Well, Commander O'Hare is going to get a new plane." Shortly after, he and his plane disappeared when he was leading a fight with two Japanese bombers. They named the Chicago airport O'Hare in memory of him.

I was working one evening—because I always worked—and all of a sudden I heard some of the guys in the hanger hollering, "Hey Lou! The officer of the day is outside the hanger in the jeep. There's some Marine with him. And he's calling your name!" I went over, and the officer points to the Marine and asks, "You know this guy?" I said, "Sure do, that's my brother!" The officer tells me very seriously, "Well, right now he's injured. He was hit at Iwo Jima. He's stationed at Aloha Hospital and he's got some time, if you've got time." I told him I was on duty, but he talked to my chief and got me liberty and took me into town. My brother and I sat a spell and talked, and that evening he took the bus back to the hospital and I went back to base.

All my brothers and I were in the service at the same time. One went up in the Army and did severe fighting with General Patton. Another was on a destroyer in the Pacific Theater. There was the Marine who got injured in Iwo Jima. The one thing that got us angry, all us boys, is that our youngest brother was drafted. I went to the draft board and tried to explain to them that there were four of us already in service, and that my mother was all alone, but they never listened, they took him in. But the war ended shortly after that. My mother's prayers were answered: we all made it home.

On my last day, my lieutenant told me that the war was over and that I was eligible to go home on the point system.[1] He said, "But I'll make a deal with you. You're a first-class mechanic. I'll give you a chief's rating." I didn't even hesitate: "No, sir." And he said, "What do you mean, no?" I told him that I promised a young girl I would come home and we would get married. He exclaimed, "Ha! I've been married three times. Good luck to ya! I'll sign your papers, you can go home!" And I came home. And here it is sixty-four years later, and we're still together.

Aviation Machinist's Mate First Class, U.S. Navy

---

1 Following victory in Europe, the U.S. military instituted a point system to coordinate demobilization. Points were tallied based on various credits, including service time, overseas time, combat credit, and parenthood credit.

Seaman, U.S. Navy

My twin brother Eddie and I signed up for the Coast Guard at the same time in 1942. We did everything together up until the war. We ran cross-country when we were kids, and we'd always win at the same time. At the finish line, they would say, "Which one are you, Buddy or Eddie?" But he got a call from the Coast Guard and I didn't, so I said, "Aw hell, I'll join the Navy." Ten days after I left for training in the Great Lakes, my Coast Guard papers arrived.

I went through ten major battles on the decks of the USS *Wichita* and USS *Washington*, so I was a busy guy![1] Kamikazes shooting, submarines shooting. I've got a big dent in my skull from kamikaze shrapnel. We were in Tarawa, Midway, Saipan, the Philippines, Iwo Jima—and the last place we went was Nagasaki. We were sent in to patrol the city. It was only a month after the bomb; we shouldn't have been there.[2] Everything looked like white sugar. The Navy put negatives on our bodies and said, "Well, we want to see if the atomic energies up there will bother you fellas." And so we wore these negatives—they were like the negatives for old-fashioned film. When we got through, they'd just throw them in a freakin' barrel to analyze later. I don't know if they ever did.

Bert Melvin (left) 1942.

I had some bad experiences. So many people were killed in Okinawa, they sent us sailors ashore to help bury them.[3] There were dead little kids in the streets. Chickens, pigs, horses—all dead. We had to dig holes and use a tractor to bury them in a mass grave. In Saipan and Guam, the poor ladies were jumping off cliffs with their babies. I think the Japanese told them we were going to rape them. I happened to be on lookout station and watched them through my binoculars—I'll never forget it, watching those poor people. And in the Philippines, I saw the terrible things done to our men—hanging them in trees, letting them bleed to death, cutting off their extremities. I hated the Japs for years later. But it wasn't the Japanese people, it was the government.

I think one of the saddest things for me was when we buried fourteen guys off of my ship. Each man was wrapped up in canvas, and at the bottom of the canvas they put an empty five-inch shell for weight. The ship slowed down, we had destroyers on either side of us, and I swear to God that I can still hear them splash as we dropped them in the water. I'll never forget that. All young kids.

During the war I wrote to my mother by V-mail.[4] You couldn't write certain things. Like when we went to Nagasaki, we released nine thousand prisoners of war, and a lot of them had been there for five years. Some of them had no legs, some of them had no arms. Scabs, bugs in them, really screwed up. I met two boys from Massachusetts, and even though you weren't supposed to correspond for any POWs, I did. I don't know how I didn't get caught, but I wrote their parents a letter telling them they were safe and that they'd been in prison for years.

When I got home to Massachusetts, they put us in a building and kept us there for two weeks. Why they did that, I don't know. But I was stuck there for two weeks while my mom and family were twenty miles away. While I was in the Pacific, my brother helped capture a German radio station in Iceland. That's where he lost three of his fingers in an engine room accident. I felt bad about his hand, but it sure was beautiful to see him again.

---

1 The USS *Wichita* was a heavy cruiser commissioned in 1939. *Wichita* entered the Pacific Theater in 1943 and participated in the Guadalcanal campaign, the invasions of the Marshall Islands and Leyte, and ultimately the occupation of Okinawa, before assisting in the repatriation of veterans following the war's end.

The USS *Washington* was a *North Carolina* class battleship that served in both the Atlantic and Pacific, including in the naval Battle of Guadalcanal, a significant victory for the Allied forces over the Japanese Imperial Navy.

2 On August 9th, 1945, at 11:02 (JST), the atomic bomb codenamed "Fat Man" was detonated over Nagasaki, Japan, by the United States. It was the second of the only two nuclear weapons to ever be used in warfare and was the third manmade nuclear explosion.

3 See pg. 152, note 2.

4 V-mail stood for Victory mail, a system that used microfilm and special letter sheets to transfer mail between U.S. soldiers and the homefront. Correspondence was reduced to fit onto microfilm, thereby saving significant amounts of cargo space, and was then increased to regular size upon reaching its destination.

WW II
MEDALS EARNED BY
US NAVY
BERT MALVIN
DISABLED

BATTLE OF MIDWAY

KNOW YE, THAT: L. D. McDougal
performed faithfully on behalf of God and
country while serving on Midway Island
from June 4, 1942 to June 7, 1942

BLANDA A.F
51056307
ROCHESTER

Opposite: **Lou BLANDA, Private Second Class, U.S. Army** Above: **Andy BROWN, Lieutenant Junior Grade, U.S. Navy**
Preceding spread: **Robert E. DIRKES, Radio Technician, U.S. Navy; L. Don McDOUGAL, Corporal, U.S. Marine Corps**

"When we packed up and set off for Okinawa, we heard the war had ended and that Japan had surrendered. For the first time, after two years, we all began to think about coming home. Of course, we had to wait our turn, which turned out to be last."

— Edgar COLE

52

Edgar COLE

I ENROLLED IN A PROGRAM AT SAN Louis Obispo to be trained as a machinist. I could have been trained as a welder, but being a machinist appealed more to me because I'm very mathematical. I went on up to San Francisco thinking I could get a job, but I was told that I was the wrong color. I was a yo-yo between the Navy shipyard and the union administrator until the union asked me, "Do you speak Spanish?" I did a little. They stamped my form and said, "Okay then, you're going to be Cuban."

I was born and raised in Dallas, so I was familiar with this situation. I was either not hired at all or hired below my experience and capability. But I had a lot of pride in being a Cole. It was a well-known name in Texas, because most of my family members were college presidents, high-school principals, and teachers. So my dad brought us up with that feeling; he'd say, "You are a Cole!" To me, struggle was not new. I didn't expect life to be easy, because it never had been. I was an excellent student in high school, so I never felt intellectually inferior.

After working in the Navy shipyard about nine months, I got my draft notice. I went to report for duty in this huge auditorium. There were hundreds of guys there and four men sitting at a table. They called a few names and said, "You're in the Army." And then they called a bunch of other names and said, "You're in the Navy." I found myself left standing alone with about three other guys. I thought, "Uh-oh, What have I done wrong? Am I at the right place? Did I come on time?" Eventually I was called over to a table, and one of the men said to me, "You are in the Marines." Well, honestly, I'd never heard of the Marines before in my life. All I knew was Army/Navy. So when he said you're in the Marines, he didn't get a reaction. He repeated it louder. But I didn't know what the big deal was. He said, "Sit back, lad," and slammed this big brown envelope on my chest. "Report for duty in thirty days!"

The envelope had a date to report and some train tickets. I got on the train and went to Washington D.C.—and that's when the hell started. I had to change trains in D.C. to go south to a segregated base in North Carolina. There was only one coach for "colored," and it was completely packed. So I panicked. I had to get on that train and the conductor wouldn't let me on. I showed him my orders. He said, "I don't care about those orders, boy, you're not getting on this train, your coach is filled!" I spotted an MP, I ran up to him, and said, "They won't let me on the train. I've got to report for duty for the

DESCRIPTION OF REGISTRANT

Race		Height (Approx.) 5'8"		Weight (Approx.) 165		Complexion	
		Eyes		Hair		Sallow	
White						Light	
		Blue		Blonde		Ruddy	
Negro	X	Gray		Red		Dark	
		Hazel		Brown		Freckled	
Oriental		Brown	X	Black	X	Light brown	
Indian		Black		Gray		Dark brown	X
				Bald		Black	
Filipino							

Other obvious physical characteristics that will aid in identification ----------

U. S. GOVERNMENT PRINTING OFFICE 16—21631

Edgar Cole's draft registration card.

An unofficial certificate awarded to sailors after passing 180° longitude.

Marines." He said, "You're not in the Marines, boy!" I said, "Here are my orders. Here are my orders." Eventually he snatched them out of my hand and opened them up and said, "I'll be damned! You are in the Marines!" Then he made them stop the train.

It was in '42, and they didn't want African Americans in the Marines. They fought it every way they could, saying we were cowards and that we raped women and all kinds of stuff they could throw at us to get the government to agree with them. It literally took an act of Congress to tell the Marines: you're going to accept African Americans whether you want to or not. The Marines picked a place for us named Montford Point where they could train us well away from the white Marines.[1]

When the Marines accepted African Americans, they said, "Okay, but we're only going to take ten thousand." Congress said, "All right, how many of those are going to be for combat?" And the Marines said, "Well, none. They can't be trained for combat." Congress said, "I'll tell you what. Why don't you take two thousand. If you can't find two thousand out of ten, then you come back and let us know and we'll decide what to do about that." So they developed all these tests. Those who didn't pass—they were put into what they called depot companies or ammo companies. In other words, work battalions. The ammo companies moved ammo around on the battlefield. The depot companies unloaded ships. So they thought that was kind of the natural order of things, that African Americans were supposed to do the work for the others. Well, they agreed with Congress that they would organize two combat outfits. The first was the 51st Anti-Aircraft Battalion. The second was the 52nd Anti-Aircraft Battalion. Because of my high marks in school, I was assigned to headquarters communications in the 52nd.

We were stationed in the Marshall Islands. My headquarters unit was dug underground in the middle of the island. We had machine guns, 40mm and 90mm. The big guns were coastal artillery to defend against submarines and the 40mm defended against aircraft. Even though I wanted to be on the guns, I had training in radio operations so my main job was to monitor Japanese radio frequencies.

When we packed up and set off for Okinawa, we heard the war had ended and that Japan had surrendered. For the first time, after two years, we all began to think about coming home. Of course, we had to wait our turn, which turned out to be last. By the time we got back to the U.S., people were tired of saying, "Welcome home!" The enthusiasm was obsolete.

It would have been nice to make a career in the Corps, but at that time they didn't accept the idea of having 'colored' officers. Eventually Congress said, "Look, you have to allow somebody to become an officer." So they gave us the test, and of course we passed it with no problems. They picked a fellow named John Rudder. This is a name that most people have never heard of, that you won't find in most history books, but he was the first African American commissioned officer.

He was my instructor and taught me everything I knew about radio communications at that time.

The last time I saw John Rudder, he was in Washington D.C., passing out leaflets about integration and fair play. I remember talking to him, and I said, "Why are you doing this? You know, you could be doing so much right now!" He said, "Well, I'm fighting for a cause. I'm fighting for equal opportunity."

---

1 Montford Point was the location of the Marine barracks that housed the first African American Marines, following President Roosevelt's Executive Order No. 8802, preventing discrimination in all branches of the armed services.

Corporal, U.S. Marine Corps

Gil MOJADO

I WAS BORN ON THE PALA INDIAN Reservation on September 11th, 1925. Life was quiet. When we were young, the government didn't want our parents to talk to us in our own language. My grandmother was the head cook at my school, and she would get fired if she spoke to me in her native tongue. I guess I grew up feeling like I was like every other American.

During World War II, I enlisted like so many other eighteen-year-old kids across the country. They sent my outfit to the Marshall Islands for eighteen months when the war was slowing down. I was stationed on the island of Enewetak, and I drove around on a speedboat.[1] Every time a new ship would come in, I would meet it. I drove people back and forth from ships to beaches. Essentially, I was a water taxi.

My life during the war was mellow. I'd take the pilots out deep-sea fishing. I met Indians from other reservations and befriended a lot of guys, but I never did go down and patrol with them. They wanted to take me out. One pilot wanted me to go on a bombing mission, but I couldn't do it. I hate to admit it, but I thought, "Oh my god, I might not come back!" I was one of the lucky ones. All of us right there on the base were. It was so calm, because they had captured most of those islands already. We saw the positive aftermath of what the men before us fought for.

We had a little *biergarten*. I did a lot of fishing. We traded stories. Outside of that, there wasn't much entertainment. I suppose the officers liked me, because they tried to encourage me to stay in the Navy when the war ended, but I wanted to go home to the reservation. I missed my grandmother—whom we called "Big"—and my mother. I was ready to go back to trade school, where I mastered carpentry, painting, and cooking.

When I returned, I was diagnosed with tuberculosis. Overseas, we lived in these two-story barracks—Quonset huts. On many nights I could feel something, like needles shooting in my hands, and I couldn't figure out what it was. So one night I said, "I'm going to stay up late and see what this is." These big rats were chewing the outer skin on my fingers! The doctors back home told me that's what caused the tuberculosis.

I had to spend two and half years at the veteran's hospital in San Fernando Valley. My lung is still half collapsed, so I am on disability. But the thing is, I'm eighty-four. I still live on my reservation and am surrounded by my family. I can still see, drive—I'm the boss of my own life.

Petty Officer Third Class, U.S. Navy

---

1 The Enewetak atoll, located in the Marshall Islands, was occupied by the Japanese until U.S. forces captured it in January 1944. Following the war, it was used by the U.S. for nuclear testing.

UNITED STATES
NAVY

Signalman, U.S. Navy

I STARTED OUT ON A TANKER IN THE Armed Guard unit, who were Navy personnel serving on merchant ships.[1] They were the ones that brought in the ammunition, the food, the tanks, the aircraft. The merchant ships came in because the Navy didn't have enough freighters. We helped organize and protect them. Our motto was "We aim to deliver"—and we did. General MacArthur said that if it wasn't for the merchant marine fleet, we couldn't have won the war.

I had to learn international signaling, which was different than Navy code. On top of that, I was the only Mexican American signalman, and there was a bit of anxiety in the beginning—but once we started working as a team, everybody forgot who they were and did the job.

Bob Figueroa on the day of his discharge.

I became used to doing things that they didn't teach us in signal school. For instance, once we were anchored to an island in the South Pacific and I saw a cloud hovering above. At dusk, the cloud began to flash. I thought it was a lightning storm until I realized that the cloud was sending out call letters via Morse code. Every ship had four call letters, and I realized the cloud was blinking mine. They didn't teach us that in school, but I shined my light at the cloud and communicated back to the ship on the other side of the island.

Eventually, I was transferred to the USS *Tucson*, an anti-aircraft cruiser. When I came onboard as petty officer second class, right out of the Armed Guard, there was a little apprehension. I was put in charge of signal watch, and there were men on the ship that felt like they should have been assigned the job. When I thought that the signal bridge needed to be swabbed, I would tell them, "Here, you gotta swab the deck." But then I would swab right there with them. I never gave an order that I wasn't willing to follow myself. It took two weeks for everyone to warm up to me, and there were no problems after that.

The *Tucson* was part of the Third Fleet task force commanded by Bull Halsey.[2] He needed to pull off a raid off northern Japan—on Honshu and Hokkaido—and selected some radiomen that were experts at faking signals. Halsey had the *Tuscon* turn around and go south, sending fake radio signals, pretending we were the *Missouri*, which was a big battleship. We were trying to fool the Japanese into thinking we were going to hit southern Japan. Apparently it worked, because when Halsey raided the north, they had no defenses in place. After we did our job, we turned around and joined the fleet in bombarding the island.

We didn't get a medal for that, because it was a classified mission and they don't give medals for something that wasn't supposed to have happened. I did get a medal for saving a Liberty ship when we were up in the Aleutian Islands.[3] During a horrible storm, the ship rode the coast of the waves and started to crack in half. The engine room reported that it was starting to see daylight! It was foggy but I signaled relentlessly all day long and into the next day, until our Navy escort ship found us and led us to a Dutch harbor.

The men on the escort ship came onboard and wanted to meet the signal crew, to congratulate the men who did their jobs so well. Our communication officer said, "That's our crew right there." They looked at me and said, "You mean that one little guy over there, he did all that?" And he said, "Yep. We only got one signalman, and he's it."

---

1 A service branch of the U.S. Navy established during World War II, the Armed Guard was tasked with defending Allied merchant ships from enemy attack.

2 The Third Fleet was formed in 1943 and commanded by Admiral William F. Halsey during World War II, leading campaigns in the Pacific War against Japan.

3 Built by welding (rather than riveting) prefabricated sections together, Liberty ships were relatively inexpensive and easy to manufacture, and played an important role as cargo ships during World War II.

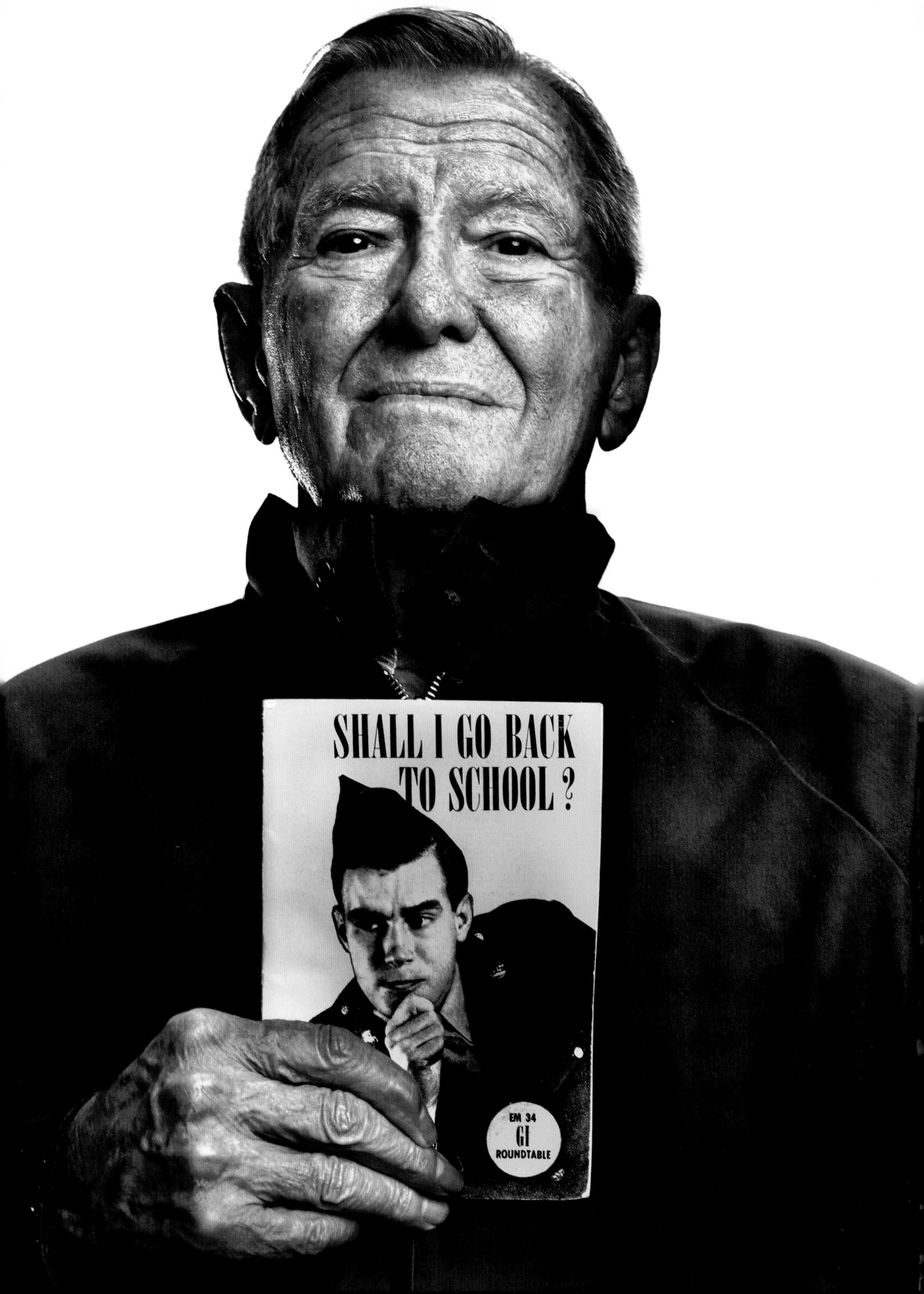
SHALL I GO BACK
TO SCHOOL ?
EM 34
GI
ROUNDTABLE

Opposite: **Henry HEIT, Electronics Technician Second Class, U.S. Navy; Sergeant, U.S. Air Force** Above: **Robert MINOR, Seaman Third Class, U.S. Navy**

I WAS TO GO TO THE ASTRONOMY building at eight o'clock and bring my roommate. Twelve or so of us were recruited out of twelve hundred students. Why me? I never knew. Maybe because I minored in German. That night we were greeted by a young Navy officer. He told us we were going to learn how to break submarine codes. He finished his speech with an admonition: "If you're not sure you want to do this, please don't stay, because if you talk about any of this, you will be shot." We all stayed. It sounded more interesting than Yale nursing! I was twenty-one when I joined the WAVES.[1]

Training lasted about six weeks. We cadets were proud of our uniforms, learning to march and salute smartly, in addition to passing serious and surprisingly difficult courses such as Naval History and Aircraft Identification. We took over an annex on the outside of Washington, DC. I started on Japanese code which was very boring. Numbers flying at us that we turned over to somebody who managed to get Japanese out of it. I requested a transfer to the German department, which was a language I knew something about. That was very exciting, because we were decoding the Enigma Machine, which the Germans used to do their submarine work.[2] Each day, the British sent us all the coded submarine messages that they had received. It was a big contest to see who could break the codes first; it felt like a game. We knew which boats were ours because the names of the German submarines that were sunk would be in the newspaper. Sometimes we had to let the Germans sink one of our ships, because if we had saved it, they would have known we were reading their code. Of course, eventually they realized, but by that point it was already the end of the war and computers were being built. Huge things, as big as a little room. One day some men came and put one into our department. Then we didn't have so much to do, just translations.

The Navy did get a little nervous about having all these women around, but they needed us. When men were trained to fly, they got sent off into combat. They needed women to transport the aircraft as it was manufactured. Women who had flown planes before joined up. A number of them were killed in action—not by the enemy, but while flying across a training ground where gunners were learning to fire. They would hit the plane when they were aiming for the target flying behind the plane. And then after the war, those female pilots were sent home because the men wanted their jobs back.

I thought in the beginning that the male sailors would resent us. But I remember once I was on a train, and this man next to me, a civilian, put his hand on my knee, and I had to push him away several times. A couple of sailors stood up and said. "You got a problem, bub?" One of them moved up and took his seat, and we never got another word out of him.

Our country was really marvelous at that time. I'd never seen it so drawn together. If you were walking down the street in your uniform, someone would offer a ride and take you where you wanted to go. It was wonderful. But if you were a man walking around in civilian clothes, women would make life hell for you! There was only one important thing in life, and that was to win the war. There are people who might think, "Well, didn't you care about those poor German sailors you were instrumental in getting killed?" And you didn't, mostly because they were the enemy and they were killing us just as fast. We worked hard, many more hours, day or night, than you do now in civilian life. I was always sleepy for three years. I never knew what my girlfriends were assigned to do. We had the fear of God put into us. We were in the business of never talking about what we did: "Loose lips sink ships!"

Lieutenant, U.S. Navy (WAVES)

---

1 WAVES was an acronym for Women Accepted for Volunteer Emergency Service. Established in 1942, the organization represented the first time since World War I that the U.S. Navy accepted a significant number of women into their ranks. Further, it was the first time women were able to achieve formal officer status, and occupations were far-ranging, including intelligence, communications, medical, and technical posts.

2 *Enigma* was the code name for the cipher device developed by the German military after World War I for encrypting their communications. The device worked by scrambling the letters of a message before transmitting, and having the receiver set their machine to an established combination that unscrambled the message upon receipt. The German Navy used an advanced version of the device, and their messages were particularly difficult for Allied code-breakers to decipher.

Chicago Daily Tribune
THE WORLD'S GREATEST NEWSPAPER
WEDNESDAY, AUGUST 15, 1945—34 PAGES
GREAT WAR ENDS
Japs Will Surrender to Gen. M'Arth
U.S.S.INDIANAPOLIS SUNK; ALL ABOARD CASUALTIES
Lost in Action After Delivering Atom Bomb Parts
ARMY TO FREE MILLIONS; CUT DRAFT QUOTAS
Jury Asks Execution of Petain
Words That Ended War
HIROHITO ACCEPTS ROLE OF PUPPET; AGREES TO CARRY OUT ALLIED ORDERS
EMPEROR SAYS ATOM BOMB MADE NIPPON GIVE UP
Truman to Proclaim V-J Day After Emissaries Complete Signing of Formal Terms

"I served on an attack transport participating in the 'magic carpet run'—bringing people and equipment home from the fighting."

George HOBERG, Lieutenant, U.S. Navy

PA 239

WHEN THEY DRAFTED ME, I WAS sent to the Army headquarters in Little Rock. I wasn't enthused about hand-to-hand combat, sleeping out in the grass, or hay rations. Certainly I would have gone just like anyone else, but I knew the Navy had beds, kitchens, and galleys, so I was pleased when they sent me there instead. They had me listed as a fireman, which meant I would work in the engine room, but when I got on the ship, they didn't have a place for me. I went all the way from Charleston, South Carolina, down to Miami, through the Panama Canal to San Diego, and then all the way to Honolulu—without a job. I called it a pleasure cruise.

Our ship, the *PGM-17*, was a converted gunboat.[1] Everyone was seasick from San Diego to Honolulu because of the storms. The men were hanging on the steps, moaning, "Go get me some crackers! Go get me some crackers!" I went back and forth between them and the kitchen passing out crackers over the nine-day journey. When we got into Pearl Harbor, I made a couple of big pans of cornbread, and boy, they liked that! No one knew anything about cooking, not a single one. So I baked and helped out in the kitchen every day. It took them a year to officially assign me to cook's duties.

We were in Okinawa two weeks before the invasion, working with minesweepers, clearing harbors that were going to be invaded.[2] About a month after they invasion, they started sending the suicide planes. And then the honeymoon was over. I felt pretty secure that the Japanese wouldn't hit us, because they always went for the big targets, and we'd shoot them. The ship ended up in the lowest part of Okinawa right up on a coral reef and couldn't get off. They put us on a six-hundred-foot-long landing craft anchored to the little island of Ie Shima.[3] I was walking on the deck toward the stern of this big wide ship, and I saw a Japanese plane coming directly toward me. It wasn't a little suicide plane, but a large fighter plane. I ran over to the other side of the ship, ready to jump in the water. I was standing there with one foot on the rail when he got shot down. I was close enough to watch the pilot scoot the cockpit back and stand up in the flames. He sat back down and crashed, missing our ship by a stone's throw.

That day at sundown we got news on the radio that Japan surrendered. There were two hundred ships in the water on the west side of Okinawa. Someone started firing anti-aircraft guns up in the air, and then guns everywhere started going off—which was a bit scary, but I celebrated just as much as any of them. Thing is, something kept bothering me a year after that day. When that plane was coming toward me, I put my hands together and prayed: "Lord, you just help me get back to Arkansas, I'll do anything you want me to do." I heard a little voice say, "Even preaching?" I shook my head, "Oh no, I can't do that, I've got to go back and farm. I can't preach." I brushed it off, but it pestered me.

When it came time to return to the States, I was on a big ship filled to the brim with men going home. I found a great big engine room with all kind of drills and saws. In the trash can, I found a piece of metal about fifteen inches long, four inches wide. It was solid, thick stainless steel and it had a little curve in it. I looked at it and thought, "What can I do, what can I make?" Well I made the cross of Christ! I laid it down on a big anvil and took a big hammer and kept hammering—put it in a vice and squeezed it. Finally got it flattened out, and then I started sawing. I used up nine brand new hacksaw blades; I wore through almost every tooth. I had to use a

George Butler after returning home from the war.

Fireman, U.S. Navy

rock to straighten up the edges. I worked for weeks. But I didn't have anything to polish it with. I put it in my duffel bag and brought it back to Arkansas, where I polished it with real fine emery cloth, enough so you could see yourself in it.

In February 1947, I gave my heart to the Lord. I was preaching in Kentucky and decided to tell the story of my cross. I was standing up in the middle of a basketball court and the light was just right and reflected on the crowd. I turned it slowly across the gym and heard *oohs* and *aahs*, and that was really touching for me to see. I've preached for sixty-two years.

1 After her commission, *PGM-17* was sent to the Pacific Theater and was involved in the Battle of Okinawa. During the first days of the battle, *PGM-17* spotted and destroyed several Japanese mines with small-arms fire. *PGM-17* spent the month of April and the beginning of May 1945 scouting and destroying mines, offering assistance to disabled and damaged ships, running supplies, and fending off kamikaze attacks.

2 The Battle of Okinawa was the last major battle of the Pacific War. The largest Allied amphibious assault, it lasted from April to June 1945, with the objective of securing a base of operations within striking distance of mainland Japan. It resulted in one of the highest casualty rates of any World War II conflict, with more than one hundred thousand Japanese and fifty thousand Allied casualties, as well as more than one hundred thousand civilian casualties.

3 The island of Iejima, also called Ie Shima, was the major starting point for the surrender of Japan in World War II. The surrender preparations started on August 17th, 1945, when Japanese emissaries traveled through Ie Shima to Corregidor to meet with General MacArthur's staff.

Above: **George KOSTELNY, Corporal, U.S. Army** Opposite: **Bob BROWN, Signalman Second Class, U.S. Navy**
Following spread: **Bob SPITLER, Aviation Chief, Radioman, U.S. Navy; Carl SPALDING, Ensign, U.S. Navy**

Four Standout Features in YOUR Sunday
New, Unusual World Map
Polar projection map shows importance of Alaska. All should clip and save it.
PICTORIAL REVIEW
Japs in Aleuts Menace U. S.
How Japs establish bases on the Aleutians, fortify, expand and INCREASE them!
PICTORIAL REVIEW
Auditing the Demagogues
In a revealing article, Merryle S. Rukeyser X-rays the demagogues on national economy.
PAGE 8, PART I
Belgian
GREATEST USED CAR DISPLAY IN THE WEST
Always in EXAMINER WANT ADS
NO. 241
CHARACTER QUALITY
Los Angeles Examiner
AN AMERICAN PAPER FOR THE AMERICAN PEOPLE
AMERICA FIRST!
ENTERPRISE ACCURACY
THE GREAT NEWSPAPER OF THE GREAT SOUTHWEST
Examiner Telephone RIchmond 1212
Giant of Journalism
LOS ANGELES, SUNDAY, AUGUST 9, 1942
Examiner Building, 1111 S. Broadway
Six Sections—Part 1
JUGGERNAUT
INTO
ROLL

I ALWAYS FELT THAT I'D LIKE THE Air Force, but I worked in the ladies' hat business. The Army didn't take beginners at thirty years old and teach them how to fly. I had to go to Canada and train with the Royal Canadian Air Force. I was there about five months, and my plane flipped over on one of my runs. I had bad eyesight. I flunked out and was sent back to the United States. So what happened next? I was recruited into the Air Corps.

I got my papers stating that I was assigned to fire control, which meant I would deal with taking care of bombs, determining what bombs to load when. There are different bombs for different things. I even learned the chemical composition of them. I went to school to learn all of this, and they made me a sergeant.

I was in the 469th Bombardment Group. We used to fly from India to China, over the Himalayas, over what they called "the Hump."[1] We were supplying the Chinese and bombing the Japanese who were stationed there. The Himalayas were so high, it wasn't very effective. From there we went to Australia, and eventually to Tinian, where we had better access. It was a wonderful island, Tinian. The weather was beautiful and we used to go swimming every day. I loved it there. Someday I hope to go back. I'm ninety-nine now, so there's still time.

The only problem with Tinian was that our men were getting killed at night, sometimes in their sleep. At first we didn't even know who was doing it. We found out it was the Japanese; they were deep in the hills and hiding in the caves. They were essentially prisoners on that island—they had nowhere to go, but they held out. And sometimes they'd sneak out at night and kill people.[2]

The A-bomb was sent to Japan from that base on Tinian.[3] I was told to watch it, but I didn't know it was what it was. They put it in the plane and took off, and away it went. So many people were killed. But that was war. That's what we call war. When I came back home I went back into business, and that's exactly where I remained the rest of my life. I never want to see a bomb or hear of a bomb again.

Sergeant, U.S. Air Force

---

1 The loss of Burma to Japan in March 1942 severed the "Burma Road," the route the Allied military had been using to supply Chinese troops. Consequently, an alternate route over the Himalayas—dubbed "the Hump"—was utilized. This dangerous pass over the mountains saw over seven thousand tons of supplies cross it each month, and it claimed the lives of more than a thousand Allied soldiers before the end of operations in China.

2 The island of Tinian was a strategic point in the U.S. military's island-hopping Pacific campaign. U.S. forces secured the island in August 1944, but despite having suffered heavy casualties, several hundred Japanese soldiers entrenched themselves in the jungle and held out. Some did not surrender until the end of the war, on September 4th, 1945.

3 At one point the busiest airbase in the war, Tinian is best remembered as the launching point of the bombers *Enola Gay* and *Bockscar*, which dropped atomic bombs on Hiroshima and Nagasaki, respectively.

"I was a part of a gas warfare unit in Sydney, gas-proofing uniforms, and eventually worked on the trigger for the atom bomb."

Roger MOORE, Technician Fifth Grade, U.S. Army

We had no idea what the Manhattan Project was, nor did we know what other groups were doing anywhere else in the Air Force.[1] Later on, we learned that a bunch of scientists were working on the development of the bomb in Los Alamos, New Mexico. In Oak Ridge, Tennessee, they had built a tremendous plant to produce uranium. There was a big plant up in Richland, Washington, to produce plutonium. But the productions were actually very, very limited by the time that we were ready to drop the bomb. General Groves was in charge of the Manhattan Project and kept things pretty secret. We were assigned the codename "Operation Silverplate" and told we were going to work on a "gimmick."[2]

My unit had fifteen airplanes and I was a co-pilot on one of them. We had spent more time with B-29s than any other crews in the military. When they sent us to Utah to train, the new B-29 was fresh off the production line and was equipped with pressurized cabins and bigger fuel tanks. They could fly for sixteen hours without being refueled. No armament and no extra protection for the crews—it was entirely stripped down in order to fly higher and faster than anything the enemy had at that time.

On our first five missions in Japan, we dropped high explosive Fat Man bombs on industrial targets such as aircraft and engineering plants. They share the same name and weight (ten thousand pounds) as the Nagasaki bomb.[3] Our sixth mission was strange because we took off without a bomb. We were told to fly over Nagasaki and report the weather back to the *Enola Gay*, a plane flying one hour behind us. There were two other planes assigned to similar reconnaissance missions, one went to Kokura and another went to Hiroshima. All three targets were clear that day.

Raymond BIEL

We knew something big was happening because our plane was parked on the runway right next to the *Enola Gay*. All the floodlights were shining on her, and photographers were taking pictures. We took off at 1:30 a.m., and she took off at 2:30 a.m. Two other planes accompanied her: an instrument ship to test the bomb as it fell and a photography ship. The photographer must have been new, because he forgot to take the lens cap off the camera that day. No pictures of the atomic bomb being dropped on Hiroshima were taken.[4]

We landed back at our base on Tinian, nine hundred miles from Hiroshima, and we shortly heard that President Truman had made an announcement: Hiroshima had been destroyed by a single bomb, and if Japan didn't surrender, other cities would get total destruction. We felt the war was going to be over in a few days, and we all started celebrating. We marveled that this was going to completely change the way war was fought—it only took one plane to destroy an entire city when it had taken three hundred planes to destroy Tokyo just a month before. Quite a change. We were thankful to be a part of the mission.

I give speeches to high-school students every year about the atomic bomb. They are usually seniors who are learning about the history of the Second World War. They always want to know how I feel about killing all those people. Here's what I tell them: You are pretty remote when you are flying at thirty thousand feet through a clear blue sky. Everything is very quiet. There's a strange sense of freedom at that altitude and a disconnect from what is happening on the ground. You've been training for a year for this mission and—you are just doing your job.

Second Lieutenant, U.S. Army Air Forces

---

1 The Manhattan Project was a codename for the development of the first atomic bomb, led by the United States, with participation from the United Kingdom and Canada. Specifically, this term describes the project between 1942 and 1945, under the direction of the U.S. Army Corps of Engineers and General Leslie Groves.

2 The U.S. Army Air Forces participation in the Manhattan Project was termed Silverplate, and referred in particular to the development of the B-29 bombers used to carry and drop atomic bombs, as well as the training and operations of the B-29 flight crews.

3 "Fat Man" is the codename for the atomic bomb that was detonated over Nagasaki, Japan, by the United States on August 9th, 1945, at 11:02 (JST). It was the second of the only two nuclear weapons ever to be used in warfare, and was the third manmade nuclear explosion. It is estimated that by 1946, seventy thousand people had died as a result of the blast, fire, and ensuing radiation.

4 The atomic bomb dubbed "Little Boy" was released by the bomber *Enola Gay* and detonated over the city of Hiroshima on August 6th, 1945. It is estimated that by 1946 one hundred and forty thousand people had died as a result of the blast, fire, and ensuing radiation.

JAMES L KELSO

To you who answered the call of your country and served in its Armed Forces to bring about the total defeat of the enemy, I extend the heartfelt thanks of a grateful Nation. As one of the Nation's finest, you undertook the most severe task one can be called upon to perform. Because you demonstrated the fortitude, resourcefulness and calm judgment necessary to carry out that task, we now look to you for leadership and example in further exalting our country in peace.

Harry Truman

THE WHITE HOUSE

Opposite: **James KELSO, Navigator, U.S. Army Air Corps** Above: **Morty JACOBS, Private First Class, U.S. Army**

I JUST GOT OFF DUTY FROM DOCtor's Hospital that morning in NYC when they aired on the radio that WWII had ended. My friend, Lucille, and I ran off to Times Square to celebrate, and moments after I exited the subway, a sailor grabbed me and kissed me. I did not know my picture was being taken. The sailor and I parted ways quickly and I told my friend, "Well, I'm glad to see his libido is still there!" He fought for me—I couldn't deny him the kiss. I walked a little distance and then a soldier kissed me! It was good to see them celebrating and kissing girls, but two kisses were enough for me and we left.

I saw the picture in the following issue of *LIFE* Magazine and was embarrassed.[1] I didn't tell anyone. I didn't want to make a public announcement. I kept my head in the school books and moved on. Thirty or so years later, after I moved to California, I told a girlfriend, and she kept urging me to get a copy of that photograph. *LIFE* was using the photograph as an advertisement to subscribe to the magazine. I wrote the famed photographer, Alfred Eisenstaedt: *I'm the nurse in the photo*. And he wrote me back, *When I go to heaven that's the picture that I will be remembered for!* He flew out to California to see if it was true. I picked him up at the Beverly Wilshire in my red Cadillac convertible, and when I got out of the car, he recognized me as the nurse—"How could I forget those legs?" Eisie and I became very good friends until he passed at the age of 98.

After I moved to Los Angeles in 1947, I became a school teacher. I taught kindergarten, first, and second grade, and I just loved it. I retired in the late 70s but a few years ago, I was asked to help children learn about the Second World War. I was very interested in the experiences of young children. Development starts at a very early age. I trained as a nurse at a psychiatric hospital for two years and I also went to graduate school at UCLA after the war and became a social worker. Today there are a number of kids who have no clue about World War II. Meanwhile, the veterans are supposedly dying one every ninety minutes.

The way the project works is that children meet with or write a letter to a veteran. They've been taught how to digitally record the interviews and are motivated to ask lots of questions: Where were you? Why did that happen? How did it feel? So far they have archived about a thousand of those stories. I find this amazing, because they're meeting with somebody who is three generations older and getting to hear what happened through their unique perspectives. Consequently, they are learning what war is about. It's one thing to read about it, and another to hear about it from the mouths of the people who were there. So far it has been thrilling for them. I truly believe a big space in their lives is being filled.

Just for children to attend public events for Veterans is educational. I've appeared as grand marshall of many veteran parades across the nation. Recently, I unveiled a twenty-five-foot statue of the kiss in San Diego next to the Midway warship. Hundreds and hundreds of people—teachers, children, youth leaders, veterans organizations—showed up. Some came from two and three hours away. They were all there to celebrate history, and I think that is tremendous.

---

1 Alfred Eisenstaedt's photograph "V-J day in Times Square" captured an iconic moment of post-war celebration in America. Originally published in *LIFE* Magazine, the photo depicts a sailor kissing Edith Shain in her nurse's uniform, in New York City's Times Square on August 14th, 1945. The image instantly became a cultural icon and represents the end of WWII and the beginning of the Baby Boomer generation.

Nurse, U.S. Army

"My publisher once told me, 'Sam, all this work you've done is on freedom. Why don't you write a piece on what freedom is?' So I went to the Oxford dictionary, and freedom has about eight different aspects. But the one that I remember was openness."

— Sam FINK

MUSSOLINI
DUX
US ARMY
REST
CENTER
No doubt. here about who lost .....

Sam FINK

I WAS TWENTY-NINE THEN. FATHER of a little boy—Mace was his name. I was married in 1940, and married men were exempt from the draft. Then I had a little boy, which made me more exempt. I remember taking a walk with my wife Adelle and saying, "God, this thing with Hitler and the Nazis. I think I've got to join the Army." She said, "Hold your horses. We've got a family now. When they want you, they'll call you." In 1944, the war in the Pacific was not going well and they had to draft fathers. Then things changed and fathers were exempt again. I breathed a sigh of relief, and Adelle was happy. But in 1945, the war in Europe was going badly and I was drafted.

Franklin Delano Roosevelt died in April 1945, while I was taking basic training in Georgia. Right when I finished training, the war in Europe ended. The Nazis surrendered. But they didn't send me home. They sent me to relieve the soldiers who had been there. I was assigned to the 88th Infantry Division in the little town of Cave del Predil, near the Austrian border. I wound up with a handful of guys sleeping in an attic. I thought, "Well, this is where I'm going to be for a long while until I get enough points to go home." It was pretty comfortable, and I had a sketchbook.

When I became a father, I worked in an art studio and wanted to be an art director—a layout man. In the Army I worked on maps. The assignment of the Eighty-Eighth Infantry Division was to station the troops along the border of Venezia Giulia—the line that separated Italy from Yugoslavia.[1] We were to keep the peace until the United Nations took the case and determined which of the two nations would get which towns. I was stationed seventy-five miles from Trieste, which was the jewel town.

The 88th was nicknamed the "Blue Devils" and sported a blue cloverleaf patch. Our neckpiece was a blue kerchief tied and fluffed in the shirt. A colonel who worked for the *New York Times* was the public relations manager of the division's newspaper. He ran an article announcing a contest for somebody to design a Thanksgiving card to be printed for the soldiers to send home. It had to say something like, "Dear Parents, we're celebrating Thanksgiving! We're getting real turkey!" That was my world before I was drafted, so I submitted a couple of sketches.

Eventually the word came from the colonel that he wanted me to finish the artwork. I was temporarily assigned to Gorizia, where the printer was located. My friends' advice was, "Screw up. Don't do it well. If you do it well, you'll never come back." But I didn't know how to screw up. I did it well, and it was a success. They transferred me down to a section in the division called G3. G1 was finance, G2 was intelligence, and G3 was plans and operations. I met Colonel Jim Tyler, a West Pointer. He took a fancy to me. All the men were heading back home, and because this Tyler liked me, as soon as a guy left, I'd get promoted. Tyler would say, "Fink, this guy's going home. You're going to be a corporal tomorrow." Two stripes sewed on. Raise in pay—$21 to $45 a month. Eventually, I wore six stripes as a master sergeant and was paid $200 a month—which I sent home to my wife.

I used to go around the town and draw anything I wanted. I made an assignment to myself to draw the interior of stores. Little stores—the candy store, clothing store, pharmacy. I filled a notebook with these. When I went to the flower shop, the man was so pleased at my sketch, he took out his rubber stamp, stamped it in the book, and wrote the date. When I went to the phar-

Sam and Adelle on their wedding day in 1940.

One of Sam Fink's sketches, made while stationed in Italy.

macy and they saw what he did, they took their stamp and wrote the date. In the end I had about seven or eight stamps. The Italian people were warm and openhearted. People stopped and said hello. It's an attitude. "Hello" is beautiful.

In 1961, I was a head of the art department in the Chicago office of Young and Rubicam. I had a title, and along with the title came a month's vacation. Adelle arranged a trip to Europe. We landed in Italy and I brought my war sketchbook along. I said, "Let's go to Gorizia for a day." We went to visit these stores. It had been fifteen years. They were exactly the same. And the guys who owned the stores put a second stamp in and signed their names again.

In the sketchbook there was the sketch of Gorizia's castle. I said, "Adelle, there it is." She laughed and she wrote in the sketchbook: *After fifteen years, we returned to where Sam was stationed for a year and a half. We walked all around the town and we spent a lovely day in a nice restaurant.* And then she wrote: *And a wonderful thing: no child ran up to Sam and said, "Hello father, where have you been?"* She paused and punctuated it with: *Good.*

My publisher once told me, "Sam, all this work you've done is on freedom. Why don't you write a piece on what freedom is?" So I went to the Oxford dictionary, and freedom has about eight different aspects. Freedom as in civil rights, the abolition of slavery, all sorts of things. But the one that I remember was openness. To be free is to be open. And today what I'm trying to do is to be open to share my life.

---

1 Venezia Giulia is the Italian name for Julian March, a region between Italy and the former Socialist Federal Republic of Yugoslavia that both sides claimed. The disputed territories were the result of an annexation after World War I that gave Italy various portions of the Austro-Hungarian Empire. During and after the Second World War, the United States administered a portion of the region.

Master Sergeant, U.S. Army

Above: **Doris Vipond ASHE, Seaman First Class, U.S. Navy** Opposite: **Nelly KLEINER, Chief Petty Officer, U.S. Navy (WAVES)**

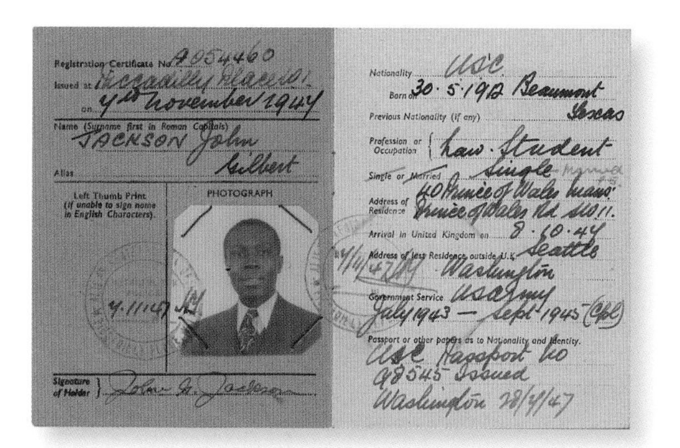
Registration Certificate No. A954460
Issued at Piccadilly
on 4th November 1944
Name (Surname first in Roman Capitals) JACKSON John Gilbert
Alias
Left Thumb Print (if unable to sign name in English Characters)
PHOTOGRAPH
Signature of Holder
Nationality USA
Born on 30·5·1912 Beaumont Texas
Previous Nationality (if any)
Profession or Occupation Law Student
Single or Married Single
Address of Residence
Arrival in United Kingdom on 8·10·44
Address of last Residence outside U.K. Seattle Washington
Government Service USArmy July 1943 — Sept 1945 (Cpl)
Passport or other papers as to Nationality and Identity.
USA Passport No 98545 Issued Washington 28/4/47

John Jackson's certificate of identification while studying in England.

I LEFT MY HOMETOWN OF BEAUMONT, Texas, and didn't return for forty years. My strongest ambition since childhood was to learn languages and see the world. The man my father worked for owned Spindletop, the first oil gusher in Texas. He used his power to promote education and a solid local justice system. Under that influence, I went to college in Chicago and moved from there to Seattle because I heard that it was the best place for blacks to work. My first job was shining shoes, but within months I became a timekeeper for the Army Quartermaster Corps.[1] I kept climbing the ladder until I was drafted—at that point I shifted into a phase of my life that I refer to as: "Two years, five months, and twenty-three days."

I was assigned to the 780th Military Police Battalion, which was all black except for the officers. In my case, black soldiers were not allowed to engage in actual fighting. We landed in Casablanca, but I spent most of my time in Algiers doing military police duties. One of my stations was the Office of Strategic Services—which is now called the CIA.[2] It was my duty to observe everything that took place at the entrance gate to the OSS headquarters. People wandered around it just like flies while I guarded the entrance. After that post, I was transferred to Marseilles, France, where I was in charge of traffic control and guarding prisoners, who were mainly incarcerated Germans.

When the war ended, all the American soldiers were impatient to get back to the States. Not me. My story isn't so much about what happened during the war, but what happened after. That's when I took action. I remained in France to learn French and got accepted into the London School of Economics, where I studied law and languages.

I met my wife at a dance in London. She was a German and Japanese beauty who wanted to find an American husband. Funnily enough, she didn't think there was prejudice in America. After we married she went by herself to take a medical examination—the final step in getting her visa. She returned very disturbed because they had rejected her due to her Japanese heritage. Having training in law, I was able to do what was proper and necessary to get her into the country, but I had to go through quite a lot of channels.

I wrote letters to people of power, starting with President Truman and Dean Acheson, the Secretary of State. I wrote that "she had been unjustly and unreasonably wronged because of an accident of birth," and that their rejection of her visa was inconsistent with a recent speech the secretary had given at the United Nations General Assembly, where he called Asia "a friend." I threw their peaceful and worldly gestures back in their faces and used their language to do so. I was able to cite the law that proved she had a right to a visa. I sent letters to senators, the NAACP, and Mrs. Eleanor Roosevelt, who was a United Nations Delegate. In fighting for her, I was fighting against the blanket of racial prejudice, and it proved to be effective. Mrs. Roosevelt and several other politicians wrote back, stating that they were considering the matter. My wife was admitted into the country shortly thereafter, and I went on to study law at New York University.

---

1 The Quartermaster Corps is a service branch of the U.S. Army, and it includes support functions such as supply and material management.

2 President Roosevelt established the Office of Strategic Services in 1942 to perform tactical research and analysis of military intelligence, as well as carry out clandestine espionage operations.

Corporal, U.S. Army

252
RESTRICTED
A POCKET GUIDE
TO
FRANCE

C2639861
Honorable Discharge
Series C
from the
United States Navy
This is to certify that
Franklin BRYANT
Seaman First Class USNR
Discharged from the
U. S. NAVAL PERSONNEL SEPARATION
and from the Naval Service of the
11th day of July 1946
This certificate is awarded as a Testimonial of
Obedience
R. B. Park
Lieut. (S) USNR
Discharge Officer
By direction of the
NAVPERS 660 (REVISED AUGUST 1945)

Opposite: **Charles BRYANT, Seaman First Class, U.S. Navy** Above: **Edward JENSEN, Technician Fifth Grade, U.S. Army**
Following spread: **John HETZ, Corporal, U.S. Air Force; Mario MENCONI, Sergeant, U.S. Army**

NAA
National
Aeronautic Association
Representing in the United States of America
The Federation Aeronautique Internationale
awards this
Certificate of Record
to
Marine Corps Squadron VMJ253
for
Longest Non Stop Mass Flight
of Twin-Engine Aircraft
12 R4D's with P&W R-1830 Engines
Naval Air Station, North Island, California to
Marine Corps Air Station, EWA, Hawaii
August 23-24, 1942
Elapsed Time: 15.8 hours
Final Destination: New Caledonia
on September 1, 1942
President
Contest and Record Board

Bill and his wife Audrey, 1946.

I STUDIED AERONAUTICAL ENGINEERing on scholarship at the Boeing School of Aeronautics. When I was twenty-five I was an assistant station manager for old Hanford Airlines. I knew a lot about planes, but I didn't fly them. I would go fishing, hunting, and bowling with all the Hanford pilots, and they talked me into going to flight school. I sent an application to the Army Air Corps and the Naval Aviation school at Pensacola, and I got accepted by both of them the same day. I flipped a coin that night and it came up tails—I went Navy.

After training, I joined a nucleus of pilots that made up a fourteen-plane squadron of commercial DC-3s. We congregated at the North Island Naval Air Station near San Diego.[1] We flew, equipped with sixteen hundred gallons of gasoline, from North Island to Ewa, Hawaii, on August 23rd, 1942. It was almost sixteen hours of flight time—the longest mass flight that had ever been made in the world.

We ended up going on down to the South Pacific and supplied the First Marine Division at Guadalcanal. We were based in New Caledonia, which was an island in the South Coral Sea, and we used to fly supplies into the canal—everything from drums of gasoline to ammunition and torpedoes. Then we would evacuate the wounded out to the rear areas of the New Hebrides Islands. The seriously wounded we'd take down to the major hospitals in Sydney and Melbourne, Australia. And that's how I met my wife.

I fell in love with her the minute I saw her in her giant white straw hat, sitting in the lobby of a Sydney hotel. We went on five dates over a two-month period, and I married her. I was the first Marine aviator married in Australia. The preacher told me, "Son, this marriage is binding in any country in the world." He wasn't about to have some Yankee marry an Australian girl and then leave her. Her father was also skeptical. He told her, "I don't know why you're marrying an American. You don't know what he does in the United States. He probably carries garbage, for all you know."

I was ordered back to the States with a group of pilots, and I told her to just stay there in Sydney and that I'd come back after the war and we'd decide what to do. She was impatient and decided to follow me, so she booked a ticket on a Swedish ship. Sweden was a neutral country at the time, but the ship was stopped twice by Japanese subs in the South Pacific. She was supposed to land in San Francisco, but there were subs sitting outside the gates there, so they ended up going to Vancouver.

I had written to her from North Island Naval Air Station and told her I was there, but when her ship arrived she couldn't find me. She told the ship's captain, "He stood me up." He wasn't having that, so he said, "You pick up that phone and call his father." When she talked to my dad in Minnesota, he said, "We've been waiting for you. You get on a Northern Pacific train and come here to St. Paul and I'll meet you." When I finally spoke to my dad, he just said, "Get on home, we have a surprise for you."

I still possess the two best things that came out of the Second World War. One, my wife. She was the highlight of the whole experience. The other one is the patch I wore on my jacket. By request, Walt Disney designed a patch for our Marine Air Group—the MAG 25.[2] We were known as the South Pacific Combat Air Transport. And Disney designed our patch—a boxcar with wings and the Red Cross insignia. On the patch it said *Securite'en Nuages*, which is Vichy French for "Safety in the Clouds."

---

1 Naval Station North Island, located on the San Diego Bay, was established in 1917. During World War II, it was a significant support base for U.S. forces in the Pacific Theater.

2 Organized in June 1942, Marine Aircraft Group 25 participated in campaigns from Guadalcanal and the Philippines to Iwo Jima and Okinawa, transporting cargo, ammunition, vehicles, and troops in and out of combat zones.

Colonel, U.S. Marines

"My most enduring memories can only be the bloodshed, the fear, and the resolve of myself and fellow soldiers to do what had to be done."

James BROWN, Staff Sergeant, U.S. Army

"During the Olympics, I tore Hitler's swastika flag off the Reich Chancellery. I thought, 'Boy, what a souvenir!'"

— Louis ZAMPERINI

WE WERE ALL SURPRISED BY HOW immaculate Berlin was. I've never seen a country so clean in my life. Hitler thought that bathtubs were contaminated because they would leave a ring, so during the 1936 Berlin Olympics, the Olympic Village was fully installed with showers. Of course, the whole world knew Hitler was building up a military machine, and when we got to Berlin, they had stormtroopers marching around. When we'd see them, we'd jokingly salute, saying, "Heil Hitler!" and they'd laugh and say, "Heil Adolf!" Everybody knew what was happening, but nobody would do anything about it. With Hitler it was wait and see, and everyone waited too long.

During the Olympics, I tore Hitler's swastika flag off the Reich Chancellery. I thought, "Boy, what a souvenir!" I gauged the time it would take to get past the guards and climb the pole. I was an Olympic runner, after all. But I misjudged the height of the flag and I couldn't reach it—I kept grabbing for it until I tore it off. After I started running away, I kept hearing "Halt! Halt!" I stopped when I heard a gunshot. They came up and flung me around rather rudely. When they asked why I wanted the flag, I said, "To remind me of the wonderful time I had in Germany." And of course that was the right answer and they let me keep it!

The next Olympics were supposed to take place in Japan in 1940—when I was in top shape and it was the peak of my career. When Pearl Harbor was hit, we just forgot about being athletes and decided to get involved. I ended up in the Pacific Theater flying bombers over Wake Island, Tarawa, Gilbert Island, and Makin Island.

One day while we were stationed on Funafuti, my crew was asked to search for a plane that had crashed two hundred miles away. Our plane was being serviced, but the *Green Hornet* was available—the plane nobody wanted to fly because it was a lemon. But we thought, "Well, if we don't have a bomb, we should be fine." When we got to the general area where they had reported going down, it became really cloudy. In order to see the ocean, we flew under the clouds, putting us way down to about eight hundred feet. We started to experience motor problems, and just peeled over and hit the water head-on. The three of us who survived got into my life raft. The gunner panicked and started screaming, "We're going to die!" I finally had to slap him in the face, and then he came around. Then we started our two-thousand-mile drift across the ocean.

We each had a pint of water on us, and it rained enough to keep us going. On the twenty-seventh day, we heard motors and we shot flares. As the plane came down lower and lower, we were waving our shirts and one of the kids was crying, "We're going to be rescued!" All of a sudden we heard machine-gun fire and a bullet went right between our legs and we looked up and we saw the Japanese red circle. He flew in circles, strafing us. We all got out and ducked under. Missed us by an eighth of an inch—nobody was touched by a bullet. There were fifty or so little holes in that raft. We played dead and the plane finally left.

The raft was wrinkled, and sharks swarmed around us. We got the pump out and we had to pump around the clock, we couldn't stop. The pilot would hold the bottom up while I put patches where the bullets had gone through, but they had to dry before we moved to the next one. It took eight hours to put on four patches. The tail-gunner sat there with an oar to keep the sharks from biting us on the fanny.

On the thirty-third day, the tail-gunner died. We'd done the best we could to keep him alive. Once we caught an albatross, and I cut the head off and squeezed all the blood into his mouth to give him nourishment. That kept him going for awhile. On the thirty-third day, he was actually better than the first day. He seemed sharper, more mature. In a way, in that situation, you really gain clarity, because you don't have the contamination of the everyday world—bad news, brainwashing, traffic, noise. Out there on the raft it's pure, clean air. Your mind is completely without any outside influence, and so you do a lot of meditating. That's all we did out there; we kept our minds active.

A Japanese patrol boat picked us up by the Marshall Islands on the forty-seventh day. We had each lost

Captain, U.S. Army Air Corps

about a hundred pounds. They put us on a ship and sent us to Kwajalein, an island which was known all over the Pacific as Execution Island.[1] We spent forty-three days there, and the whole time I wished I was back out on the raft. They tormented us every day. They lined us up, screamed at us, spat at us, threw rocks at us, jabbed us with sticks. Then they used us for guinea pigs, they injected us with something that made us dizzy and prickly all over and made it so we couldn't sleep at night. Then they'd wait a day and do it again.

Finally they interviewed us—six naval officers in white uniforms, gold braid. They smoked cigarettes and blew the smoke in our faces. They were eating pastries, drinking soda pop, and we got nothing unless we answered their questions. Eventually our day of execution was set. An officer from another division who followed the Olympics knew who I was. When I had crashed and disappeared, it made headlines. He told them it would serve Japan better to send me to Tokyo to make a radio broadcast. When I got there, they handed me a sheet of propaganda. I said, "No way."

Louis Zamperini with his training plane.

They sent me to a slave labor camp. And that was really brutal. Working all day shoveling coal and asphalt. Just before the war ended, a Japanese guard said that a horrible thing had happened in a city called Hiroshima. He said that cholera broke out and that it was quarantined. Ten days later we heard about an atomic bomb—what's that? Nobody knew what an atomic bomb was. They had dropped one on Nagasaki. We were up in Nagano, which was snow country in northern Japan—where the Olympics were supposed to be held.

When we were freed, we got on a train to Yokohama, and the Red Cross had Coke, doughnuts, and coffee waiting for us. As soon as we got off the trains, this journalist standing there asked, "Who's got a good story?" This buddy of mine grabbed me and said, "He does." I stood outside for forty minutes being interviewed by Robert Trumbull for the *New York Times*. I couldn't get away from the guy. When we were through, I rushed in to get my doughnuts and coffee—nothing left. I looked on the floor for just a crumb of a doughnut, just to taste it. Not even a crumb.

By the time I got back to Hawaii, the *Times* interview had broken nationwide. I was famous overnight. My mother was crying, pestering some general, wanting to know if I was okay and why I wasn't home yet. Home was in Torrance, California, but I was kind of having a ball in Hawaii. I didn't want to go home. But I got a red-letter order, and that means that you gotta respond immediately. It said, "Get your ass back here with every available dispatch." I left immediately and reunited with my family for first time in four years.

I had to meet with a psychiatrist after my experience, and she asked, "Well, how do you deal with your anxiety?" I said, "I don't have any." She said, "Everybody does." And I said, "Well, I don't." She asked, "What do you mean you don't have any anxiety—something happened, if you don't deal with it, it turns into frustration, if you don't deal with that, it turns into stress, and if you don't deal with that, it turns into chronic fatigue syndrome." And I told her, "Well, when anxiety knocks on my door, I don't let it in. The Bible says love your neighbors as you love yourself, do good to them that hate you, pray for them who despitefully use you—what am I lettin' in?"

I'm ninety-three. That is the answer to my longevity. That's the answer to a strong immune system and psychological well-being: doing good and helping people and feeling good about it. That would be the end of my book if I ever have time to write it.

---

1 An atoll in the heart of the Marshall Islands, Kwajalein was the location of a Japanese base and part of their Pacific territories before it fell to U.S. forces in 1944. It was also where nine Marine Raiders captured at the island of Makin had been taken and executed. Tried before the Naval War Crimes commission in Guam, Vice Admiral Kōsō Abe, commander of the Marshall Islands bases; Captain Yoshio Obara, commander of Kwajalein; and his police chief, Commander Hiusakichi Naiki, were found guilty of war crimes. Abe was hanged, and Obara and Naiki were sent to prison.

"World War II was our duty. We didn't start it, but we helped finish it for the world."

Bill HALL, Lieutenant Colonel, U.S. Air Force

James TOBIN, First Lieutenant, U.S. Navy

U.S.

INDEX OF VETERANS

Interviews in bold

ACKNOWLEDGMENTS

I OFFER A DEEP BOW OF GRATITUDE TO THE FOLLOWING people. Neither this book nor I would be the same without them.

Dawneen Lorance, for giving me my first chance to photograph a WWII veteran, for believing in me, and introducing me to Belmont Village. Without you, none of this would have happened.

My heartfelt gratitude to Belmont Village Senior Living for caring enough about their veterans to commission my travel to their communities throughout the United States. A special thank you to Belmont Village CEO, Patricia Will; Vice President of Communications, Jeff DeBevec; Director of Public Relations, Amy Self; Executive Vice President of Operations, Rob Rollans; Senior Vice President of Sales, Carlene Motto; Public Relations associates, Julie Walke of Walke Communications in California and Betsy Shepherd of Connected Communications in Chicago; all the employees at the Belmont Village communities across the country for helping organize the photo shoots and galleries.

Hampton Sides, I am so happy to share these pages with an author who feels as passionately about veterans as I do.

Peter Beren, the greatest literary agent and businessman, thanks for being patient with me.

Veronica Kavass, for your long hours of dedication, patience, and your gift for making people want to share their stories. Thank you, thank you!

The entire staff of Welcome Books—I could not ask for a better publisher. It is your sense of family and 'welcoming' attitude that makes you all such a wonderful team. I am exceptionally appreciative to my publisher Lena Tabori, for passionately working so hard and understanding the importance of my project; Associate Editor and renaissance man, Gavin O'Connor, thank you for your endless encouragement and doing everything imaginable for the book; Associate Publisher Katrina Fried, for your enthusiasm, persistence, and your miraculous skills with words; Art Director Gregory Wakabayashi, your preeminent design skills that no one can match, thank you for making the book so beautiful; and to everyone else at Welcome for their relentless hard work.

Everyone at Sandbox Studios—for showing me how to get my hands dirty in the photography industry.

My professors at Cal Poly San Luis Obispo Art and Design Program, for pushing me to do my best; and my fellow classmates for being there for me.

Silas and Julia King, for helping me get work when I first moved to LA, and your support and critique.

Ed Aiona, for teaching the correct direction of holding a light meter.

Scott Council and Ginger Cho, for teaching me the photography business and giving me all the used photography equipment I could ever hope for.

For their guidance, support and friendship, and advice along the way, I would like to thank: Larry Letters, Fred Stimson, Jim Mueller, the Arbuthnot Family, Rick

Bolan, Andy Mitchell, Linda Wellmerling at the Canterbury, Pat Valone at Sonoma Hills, Leisure World, Carl and Billy Wolfrom, and the Piatti Family.

Gary Zimmerman of The WWII Store Torrance, CA, I cannot thank you more for your generosity and cooperation.

Wally Petersen of Military Antiques and Museum in Petaluma, CA, I express deep gratitude for your assistance and superb collection of memorabilia.

My love, Allison Arbuthnot, for your enthusiasm, utmost support, and for being my best friend.

My dad, Robert Sanders, my first photography mentor, for opening my eyes to the world of art, and for the generous encouragement along the way.

My mom, Eva Ananias, for pushing me in school, encouraging me to dream big, and for being my spiritual counselor.

My grandparents; Eva and Roger Westberg, for all the photography books and help when I needed it; Jane and Willis Sanders, for showing me how to light a portrait with a desk lamp, giving me my first 4x5 camera, and passing on your superb photography genes; and Dave Denney, for your kind thoughts along the way.

Denney Family; Gerry, Amparo, David, Julia, and Sophie, for your patience, love, and support (*Om* to you all).

My step-mom, Michele, for making a dangerously good mudpie when I was in need of comfort.

My siblings, Ian and Brenton, for tying me up to trees and helping develop my creativity; Eva for being my buddy through the thick and thin; Colleen, Stephen, Tim, and Peter, for withstanding my teenage pranks as a funnel for creativity; Meghan and Sean, for being some of my first photo subjects.

The families of the WWII veterans, you were there to help your parents stand, and share their stories and memories. Thank you.

Above all, our WWII veterans and allies, without you, we would be living in a much different world. All veterans and soldiers who sacrifice their safety for ours, I honor and deeply thank you.

—Thomas SANDERS

Thank you to Douglas Gayeton, who introduced me to Katrina Fried and Welcome Books; to A.K., who gave me great feedback when this project first began; to the veterans I interviewed for being such great storytellers; and to my father, who taught me how to listen.

—Veronica KAVASS

Following page: **Fred WALTERS, Staff Sergeant, U.S. Army**

VFW
6158